THE **BIG** ADVENTURE

D0300707

DINOSAUR COVE™

DINOSAUR COVE™

THE **BIG** ADVENTURE

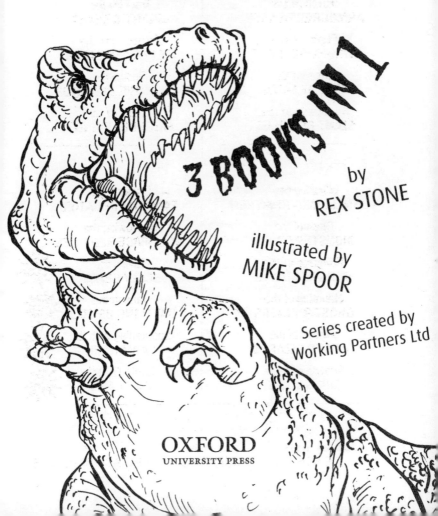

3 BOOKS IN 1

by
REX STONE

illustrated by
MIKE SPOOR

Series created by
Working Partners Ltd

OXFORD
UNIVERSITY PRESS

OXFORD
UNIVERSITY PRESS

Great Clarendon Street, Oxford OX2 6DP
Oxford University Press is a department of the University of Oxford.
It furthers the University's objective of excellence in research, scholarship,
and education by publishing worldwide in

Oxford   New York

Auckland   Cape Town   Dar es Salaam   Hong Kong   Karachi
Kuala Lumpur   Madrid   Melbourne   Mexico City   Nairobi
New Delhi   Shanghai   Taipei   Toronto

With offices in

Argentina   Austria   Brazil   Chile   Czech Republic   France   Greece
Guatemala   Hungary   Italy   Japan   Poland   Portugal   Singapore
South Korea   Switzerland   Thailand   Turkey   Ukraine   Vietnam

Oxford is a registered trade mark of Oxford University Press
in the UK and in certain other countries

British Library Cataloguing in Publication Data

Data available

ISBN: 978-0-19-279271-6

3 5 7 9 10 8 6 4

Printed in Great Britain
Paper used in the production of this book is a natural,
recyclable product made from wood grown in sustainable forests
The manufacturing process conforms to the environmental
regulations of the country of origin

CONTENTS

DINOSAUR COVE™

ATTACK OF THE LIZARD KING

by
REX STONE

illustrated by
MIKE SPOOR

Series created by
Working Partners Ltd

OXFORD
UNIVERSITY PRESS

Special thanks to Jane Clarke

To the real Jamie Morgan, with love and kisses

FACT FILE

⟹ JAMIE HAS JUST MOVED FROM THE CITY TO LIVE IN THE LIGHTHOUSE IN DINOSAUR COVE. JAMIE'S DAD IS OPENING A DINOSAUR MUSEUM ON THE BOTTOM FLOOR OF THE LIGHTHOUSE. WHEN JAMIE GOES HUNTING FOR FOSSILS IN THE CRUMBLING CLIFFS ON THE BEACH HE MEETS A LOCAL BOY, TOM, AND THE TWO DISCOVER AN AMAZING SECRET: A WORLD WITH REAL, LIVE DINOSAURS! SOME DINOSAURS TURN OUT TO BE FRIENDLY, BUT OTHERS ARE FEROCIOUS AND ... HUNGRY!

JAMIE

- **FULL NAME:** JAMIE MORGAN
- **AGE:** 8 YEARS
- **SIZE:** 1 JATOM*
- **TOP SPEED:** 10 KPH
- **LIKES:** FOSSIL HUNTING AND LEARNING ABOUT DINOSAURS
- **DISLIKES:** BEING STUCK INDOORS

Jamie's eye

Jamie's foot

Jamie's hand

*NOTE: A JATOM IS THE SIZE OF JAMIE OR TOM: 125 CM TALL AND 27 KG IN WEIGHT

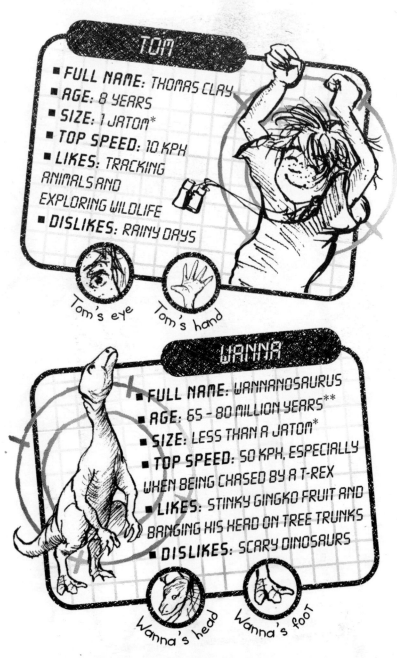

TOM

- **FULL NAME:** THOMAS CLAY
- **AGE:** 8 YEARS
- **SIZE:** 1 JATOM*
- **TOP SPEED:** 10 KPH
- **LIKES:** TRACKING ANIMALS AND EXPLORING WILDLIFE
- **DISLIKES:** RAINY DAYS

Tom's eye   Tom's hand

WANNA

- **FULL NAME:** WANNANOSAURUS
- **AGE:** 65 – 80 MILLION YEARS**
- **SIZE:** LESS THAN A JATOM*
- **TOP SPEED:** 50 KPH, ESPECIALLY WHEN BEING CHASED BY A T-REX
- **LIKES:** STINKY GINGKO FRUIT AND BANGING HIS HEAD ON TREE TRUNKS
- **DISLIKES:** SCARY DINOSAURS

Wanna's head   Wanna's foot

*NOTE: A JATOM IS THE SIZE OF JAMIE OR TOM: 125 CM TALL AND 27 KG IN WEIGHT
**NOTE: SCIENTISTS CALL THIS PERIOD THE LATE CRETACEOUS

T-REX

T-Rex's claw

T-Rex's eye

T-Rex's Teeth

T-Rex's Tail

- **FULL NAME:** TYRANNOSAURUS REX
- **AGE:** 65 – 80 MILLION YEARS**
- **HEIGHT:** 5 JATOMS*
- **LENGTH:** 10 JATOMS*
- **WEIGHT:** 200 JATOMS*
- **TOP SPEED:** 48 KPH
- **LIKES:** FRESH FLESH AND CRUNCHING BONES
- **DISLIKES:** CHEWY GREEN LEAVES AND OTHER T-REX

*NOTE: A JATOM IS THE SIZE OF JAMIE OR TOM: 125 CM TALL AND 27 KG IN WEIGHT
**NOTE: SCIENTISTS CALL THIS PERIOD THE LATE CRETACEOUS

DINOSAUR COVE

Village

Marina

Sealight Hed

12

Landslips where clay and fossils are

Muddy beach

DINO CAVE

h Tide beach line

Low Tide beach line

Sea

Smuggler's Point

'Dinosaur Cove!' Jamie ran to the cliff edge and looked down over the fence. 'This has got to be the best place on earth to find dinosaurs!'

His grandad's eyes twinkled. 'They're down there in the rocks, that's for sure. Why don't you go and have a look?'

'Fossils, here I come!' Jamie said. 'See you later, Grandad.'

Jamie scrambled down the rocky path from the old lighthouse onto the sand. He turned away from the sea and ran straight up the

beach, over pebbles and rocks, to the sludgy black mud nearest the foot of the cliff.

That was the place to find fossils.

Jamie kept his eyes fixed on the muddy rocks and every so often he bent down to pick one up. They were crumbly and broke apart in his fingers, but none of them had a fossil inside. *Maybe I should try a bigger rock*, he thought.

He spotted a large blue-grey rock with a crack down the middle and dumped his backpack on the mud beside it. He dug out his safety goggles and his fossil hammer and chisel. Then he set to work, angling the chisel

into the crack and tapping it with his
hammer. He tapped again. He tapped harder.

A stone chip pinged off Jamie's goggles as
the rock split cleanly in two.

'Treasure!' Jamie said.

Sticking out of one half of the rock was
a black spiral fossil with shiny gold ridges.
He looked at it closely. It was about the length
of his finger. But when he tried to pick it out,
it was stuck fast in the rock.

The Fossil Finder will tell me what it is, Jamie
thought. He fished in his backpack and took

out his favourite new gadget—a hand-held computer. He flipped the lid and the screen glowed with a picture of a fossilized dinosaur footprint, then the words: *'HAPPY HUNTING!'*

At the bottom of the screen, a cursor blinked. Jamie tapped *'FOSSIL SHELL'* on the small keypad, looked again at his fossil, and typed what it looked like: *'COILED ROPE'*. Then he pressed *'FIND'* and stared at the screen. A picture popped up. It looked just like the fossil in the blue-grey rock.

'AMMONITE,' Jamie read. 'A FOSSIL SHELL FROM A PREHISTORIC SEA CREATURE, COMMON IN ROCKS FROM DINOSAUR TIMES; CAN BE FORMED OF FOOLS GOLD.'

He flipped the lid shut.

'Well,' Jamie said to his discovery, 'I don't care that you're common, or that you're not real gold. You come from dinosaur times, and I'm the first person ever to see you. So you're still treasure to me!'

He pulled his goggles off, took out his new T-Rex notebook and began to sketch his first Dinosaur Cove discovery.

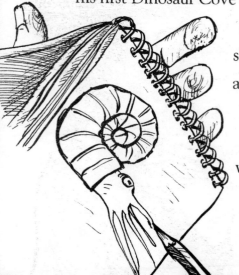

He added in the squid-like tentacles and big eye that the creature would have had when it was alive.

Suddenly, an unfamiliar voice shouted,

'BOO!'

A freckly face popped up from behind the rock. 'Gotcha! You didn't hear me coming, did you?' The boy stood up. His T-shirt and safari shorts were plastered in mud. 'Is that the new Fossil Finder?'

Jamie smiled and patted the lid. 'Latest software and everything.'

The boy pushed his curly red hair behind his sticky-out ears. 'I'm Tom Clay,' he said. 'I'm learning to track animals and I'm going to be a wildlife presenter on TV one day. Who are you?'

'Jamie Morgan,' said Jamie, 'I want to be a scientist.'

'You're new, aren't you?' Tom said.

Jamie nodded. 'I just moved here. Look! I found an ammonite.'

'Oh, ammonites,' said Tom, shrugging. 'You'll find loads of those around here.'

'I want to find a dinosaur bone,' Jamie told him. 'Dinosaurs are awesome!'

Tom looked at Jamie's notebook and laughed. 'T-Rex rules!' He put his binoculars to his eyes.

'Sometimes I pretend I'm tracking dinosaurs . . .'
His binoculars flashed in the sunshine as he turned them on Jamie.

Tom grinned. 'Hey, do you want to know a secret about Dinosaur Cove?'

'You bet!' said Jamie.

'Then follow me. We have to be quick!' Tom set off across the beach.

Jamie stuffed his fossil-hunting gear into his backpack and ran after his new friend. 'Why are we hurrying?' Jamie asked.

'The path up the cliff gets cut off at high tide,' Tom said. 'So we'll have to get back before then.'

Tom led Jamie onto a narrow path up a cliff and at the highest point on the path, Jamie stopped to look at the view. He could see Grandad fishing down on the beach.

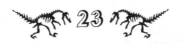

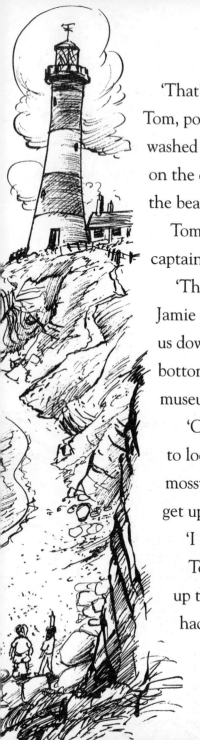

'That's my house,' Jamie told Tom, pointing to the tall white-washed tower at the top of the cliffs on the opposite side of the beach.

Tom looked surprised. 'The captain's lighthouse?'

'The captain is my grandad,' Jamie explained. 'My dad moved us down here and he's turning the bottom floor into a dinosaur museum.'

'Cool!' said Tom. He turned to look at the huge pile of mossy boulders. 'We've got to get up there.'

'I love climbing!' Jamie said.

Together the boys clambered up the boulders. Once Jamie had hauled himself onto the

huge stone at the top he asked, 'So, where's
the big secret?'

'Right behind you,' Tom told him.

Jamie spun round. Behind the boulder and
hidden from the bay was the gaping mouth of
a cave.

'A secret cave!' Jamie gasped.

CHAPTER 2

SEARCH:

'It's a smugglers' cave,' Tom told Jamie.
'It hasn't been used for a hundred years.'

Jamie stepped into the mouth of the dark
cave and dug his hand into his backpack,
pulling out his torch.

'This is where the smugglers stored their
booty,' Tom said. 'You can see the marks from
their lamps.'

Jamie flicked on his torch and shone it over
the pale rock walls. He could make out sooty
black streaks. Tom took a few more steps into

the cave and knocked on the back wall. 'It's a
dead end.'

Jamie shone his torch over the floor and
saw a spider with long, spindly legs. He
followed it in the beam as it skittered into
the corner and then disappeared into
a hole.

'It can't be a dead end,' Jamie said. 'Look!'

The hole began at the cave floor and went

up to the height of his knees. It was wide at the bottom, but very narrow at the top.

'How did I miss that?' Tom said. 'I've been in here loads of times.'

'It's big enough to squeeze through.' Jamie knelt and pushed his backpack through the gap. 'I'm going in.' He wriggled through the gap, shining his torch into the darkness.

'Wait for me!' yelled Tom.

It was colder and pitch black inside the second chamber. Jamie shone his torch over the rock walls, ceiling, and floor. There was no sign of any soot from smugglers' lamps.

'We must be the first people to come in here for hundreds of years,' Tom murmured.

'Thousands of years!' said Jamie.

'Millions!' said Tom.

'Hey, what's this?' Jamie's torchlight fell on a scoop in the stone next to his feet. He knelt down and traced his finger around the clover-shaped indent. It looked just like the dinosaur footprint on his Fossil Finder.

'I think this could be a fossil,' Jamie announced, excitement tingling through him.

Jamie rummaged in his bag and flipped open the Fossil Finder. The display picture of a dinosaur footprint glowed in the darkness. 'Yes, it's a fossilized dinosaur footprint!'

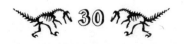

'Wow,' Tom said, looking from the screen to the cave floor. 'Those are really rare!'

Jamie saw a second scoop at the edge of the beam of light. 'Look! There's another . . . and another . . . Five altogether. They go straight into that wall of rock.'

Jamie could hardly believe it. On his very first day exploring Dinosaur Cove, he had found the fossilized tracks of a dinosaur!

Jamie carefully placed his left foot into the first print. 'It's got the same size feet as me!' He swung his right foot into the next print. Jamie grinned at Tom, who was following behind him. 'We're tracking dinosaurs! Left foot.'

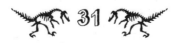

A crack of light appeared in the cave wall.

'Right foot . . . ' The light brightened as the crack widened. Jamie put his left foot forward to take another step and the crack of light got wider and brighter. He covered his eyes with his hands. When he put his foot down, the ground felt spongy.

Cautiously, he took his hands away from his eyes.

Jamie wasn't in the small dark chamber any more. He was in a sunny cave with a wall of stone behind him. The footprints were still there—only now they weren't fossils. They were fresh!

He took a step forward into the new cave, and Tom appeared behind him—right through the wall of stone!

'Where are we?' Tom asked.

'I don't know,' Jamie said, looking around at the strange new place.

Jamie walked out of the cave and the ground squelched beneath his feet. The area was thick with trees and vines, so he couldn't see very far.

33

'These trees are weird.' Jamie pulled an apricot-like fruit from a cluster hanging on a nearby branch. It smelled horrible. 'Yuck! Dare you to smell it, Tom.'

Tom took a huge sniff. 'Sick!' he gasped. Then he grinned. 'Dare you to take a bite.'

'No way!' said Jamie, shaking his head.

The ground was slimed with the stinky orange outer pulp of the fruit that had fallen off the tree. Jamie picked up a fan-shaped leaf from the tree. 'You know, I think I've seen this somewhere before.'

He dug out the Fossil Finder and typed
'FAN-SHAPED LEAF'. The next moment,
pictures of leaves appeared on the screen.
Jamie clicked on the one that looked the
same as the leaf in his hand.

'GINGKO: A LIVING FOSSIL,' he read to Tom.
*'STILL FOUND TODAY, BUT EVERYWHERE
IN DINOSAUR TIMES; SOMETIMES KNOWN
AS A STINK BOMB TREE.'*

'Too right,' said Tom. 'Let's get some fresh
air!' He pushed aside a tangle of creepers.
'What's through here?'

'Wait for me!' Jamie hurriedly sealed a few
gingko fruits into a plastic specimen bag,

stuffed them and the Fossil Finder into his backpack, and then crashed through the undergrowth after Tom.

'Careful!' Tom shouted to him from up ahead.

The ground sloped steeply and Jamie tried to slow down, but his trainers were caked with slippery gingko pulp!

'I can't stop!' Jamie yelled as he tumbled towards the edge of a cliff.

CHAPTER 3

Tom thrust out the end of a stick. 'Grab this, Jamie!' he shouted.

Jamie threw out his arm and caught hold as one foot went over the edge. He wobbled, and then steadied himself. 'Thanks! That was close!'

Jamie stepped back from the cliff edge and gazed at the landscape in front of him. A canopy of grey mist hung over a forest of brilliant emerald green. The humid air throbbed with the whirring and buzzing of insects.

'Where is this?' he gasped. Among the trees, Jamie saw a beautiful blue lagoon and beyond that was an expanse of water. 'Is that Dinosaur Cove?'

'No way,' said Tom, looking through his binoculars. 'That's an ocean.'

Ark! Ark! Ark!

The sudden noise came out of the sky behind them and Jamie turned to see a scarlet-headed bird the size of a small aeroplane swooping towards them.

'Watch out!' he yelled to Tom.

They ducked as silver-grey leathery wings swept right over their heads. Tom followed the bird with his binoculars.

'It's flying over the jungle . . . it's settling on a tree by the lagoon,' he told Jamie. 'Take a look! It's huge!'

He thrust the binoculars at Jamie. Jamie looked towards the lagoon and his jaw dropped open. He couldn't believe his eyes!

'What can you see?' Tom asked.

'I can see,' Jamie spoke carefully, 'two rhinos, but instead of one big horn, they have three. Which means,' he whispered, 'that they're not rhinos . . . they're triceratops!'

'What?' Tom said. 'Let me see!'

Jamie passed back the binoculars. 'You're right,' Tom said. 'And that huge bird is not a bird. It's a pterodactyl!'

The boys looked at each other in amazement.

'DINOSAURS!!'

they yelled together, punching the air.

'But how . . . ?' Tom stuttered.

'I don't know,' yelled Jamie. 'But we've got to get closer!'

'Over there,' said Tom. 'There's a slope down to the jungle.'

The boys scrambled and skidded down the hill, and soon their feet sank into the spongy jungle floor. Great conifers towered above them and huge ferns brushed damply against their legs as they passed. An enormous frill of purple and yellow spotted fungus caught Jamie's eye. It sprouted from a rotten tree stump.

'This is unreal!' Jamie said. But then, on the far side of the fungus, the ferns began to rustle.

Grunk.

'Did you hear that?' Jamie whispered.

'What?' Tom stood still.

The ferns swished. *Grunk.*

'That!' Jamie hissed. 'There's something there!'

Jamie and Tom ducked down behind the tree stump, and then slowly peeked out from behind the fungus.

45

The noises were coming from a plump scaly creature with a flat bony head and splotchy green-brown markings. It was standing on two strong legs, peering hopefully into a tree.

'It's a little dinosaur!' Jamie whispered.

As they watched, the little dinosaur grabbed hold of the conifer with its claws, steadying itself by digging its long tail into the ground. Then it shook the tree as hard as its short arms would allow it to. The little dinosaur's tail twitched and it grunked softly to itself.

'He's thinking,' Tom murmured.

'He's so cool!' Jamie breathed.

The dinosaur took a few steps back. He lowered his bony head and charged straight at the tree.

Thwack!

The flat top of the dinosaur's head hit the tree trunk and the conifer shook.

Thwack!

'He's strong,' said Tom.

'Do you think he's dangerous?' Jamie asked.

'I'll look him up.' Tom pulled out the Fossil Finder from Jamie's backpack, and tapped in keywords: *FLAT SKULL,' 'HEAD BUTT.'*

'WAN-NA-NO-SAUR-US,' Tom read from the screen. *'A HERBIVORE.'*

'That means a plant eater,' added Jamie.
'USES ITS HARD SKULL TO DEFEND ITSELF AGAINST PREDATORS.'

As Tom slipped the Fossil Finder back into Jamie's bag, the little dinosaur took another run up and rammed the tree again.

'He thinks the tree's a predator!' Tom stood up, laughing.

At the sound of Tom's laughter, the little dinosaur cocked his head to one side. He turned and blinked mournfully at Tom.

'You've hurt his feelings,' Jamie said, standing up beside Tom.

'Sorry, Wanna,' Tom told the little dinosaur.

The wannanosaurus blinked at Tom and then at Jamie. He took three big steps away from the tree and shifted its weight from foot to foot.

'He's revving up,' said Jamie.

'Go, Wanna, go!' the boys shouted.

The wannanosaurus put its head down and hurtled towards the tree.

Thwack!

The tree wobbled.

Plunk!

A single pine cone dropped to the ground. The dinosaur stuffed it into his mouth and looked happily at the boys. Then he wagged his tail and scurried off on his hind legs.

'Let's track him!' said Tom.

'Just a minute . . . ' Jamie carved a 'W' into the tree stump with his fossil hammer. 'So we remember where we met Wanna.'

'Now, which way did he go?' asked Jamie, as they clambered over the tree.

Tom looked around at the trampled plants. 'He disturbs the ferns as he walks on them,' Tom said. 'We can follow his trail.'

The little dinosaur's trail led to a small clearing and the boys found him standing on his hind legs, munching a leaf. He turned towards them and lowered his flat bony head.

'Uh oh,' said Tom. 'He might charge us!'

'It's OK, Wanna. We're not predators.' Jamie put his backpack on the ground and took out his bag of stinky gingko fruit.
He rolled one towards the wannanosaurus. The dinosaur sniffed at the fruit suspiciously.

'He can't possibly want to eat that,' said Tom, holding his nose.

50

Wanna looked down his snout at Tom, then he pinned the fruit between his claws and sank his teeth into it. He made grunking noises as stinky gingko juice dribbled down his chin.

'Yum yum!' Jamie grimaced as the dinosaur's long tongue slurped up every disgusting drop.

Wanna looked at Jamie. Then he looked at Jamie's backpack and wagged his tail.

Suddenly, the little dinosaur froze.

The jungle went still. Even the insects stopped buzzing. The ground trembled beneath their feet.

'Something's coming,' whispered Jamie. 'Something big . . . '

Thump!

The ground shook. Wanna dashed behind the leafy tree.

Thump!

A stronger tremor shook the ground. Wanna peeped out from behind a branch and bobbed his head up and down.

In the distance, wood was snapping and cracking. The tremors were getting stronger.

'Whatever it is, is coming our way,' Jamie said.

'Fast,' added Tom.

The boys looked at each other.

'We've got to get out of here!' Jamie yelled.

'Which way?'

Suddenly, Jamie's bag was yanked off his back. Jamie spun round and saw Wanna

charging off into the jungle, clutching it in
his mouth.

'Wanna!' Jamie sprinted after him, Tom
close behind.

The little dinosaur skidded to a halt by a
shallow stream. He turned and looked Jamie
in the eyes. Then he jerked his head towards
the stream and plunged in.

The ground shook again.

'Wanna's leading us to safety!' Jamie shouted, jumping into the stream after him.

'Clever!' Tom panted. 'The water will mask our scent.'

Wanna led them up the stream to where it trickled through a jumble of huge rounded rocks. He glanced back and leaped out of the water.

Jamie and Tom followed, stumbling and splashing. They scrambled onto the rocks and stood, dripping.

'Where's he gone?' Jamie said.

RAAAR!

Something crashed through the trees behind them. Jamie whirled round and lost his footing on the wet stone.

Tom threw out his hand, but when Jamie grabbed it both boys toppled and slid down

between two rocks. Jamie landed with a thud and found himself staring into a reptilian face.

Grunk!

Wanna greeted Jamie and Tom with slobbery licks, and Jamie was happy to see his backpack again.

'Are we safe?' Jamie whispered. 'Has that thing chasing us gone?'

The boys listened.

'I think so!' Tom breathed.

Thud!

The rocks shook.

'It's here!' Tom whispered.

Jamie peered up through the gap above his head. Instead of the trees of the jungle, he saw a dark slimy hole.

 57

Suddenly, a blast of slime flew from the hole and splattered Jamie's face.

'*Aargh!*' Jamie wiped his face. 'I think that's its nose.'

The creature lifted its head and roared.

RAAAR!

The sound rumbled around the rocks.

Jamie could see its jaws. Slithers of rotting flesh dangled from its fangs.

'Ugh! Bad breath!' Jamie gagged. 'Worse than stinky gingko fruit.'

'It doesn't look friendly,' Tom said. 'W-what is it?'

An enormous yellow eye, rimmed with bright red scales, studied Jamie through the gap in the rocks.

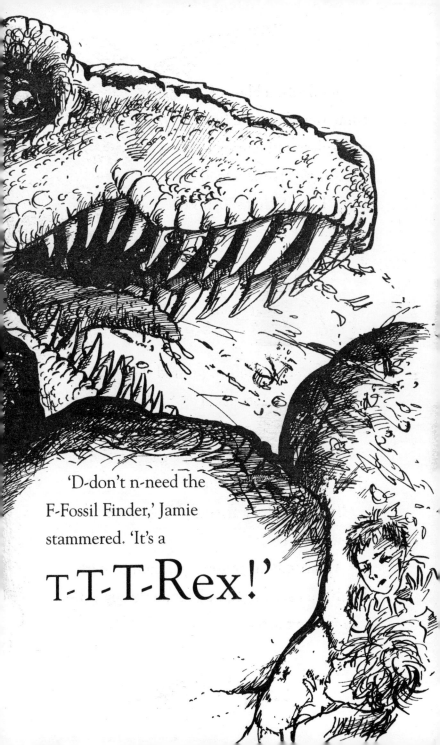

'D-don't n-need the F-Fossil Finder,' Jamie stammered. 'It's a

T-T-T-Rex!'

The eye disappeared.

'We're in trouble!' Jamie breathed.

'*Serious* trouble,' Tom said.

Suddenly, a long claw stabbed down into the crevice.

'Watch out!' Jamie yelled. He pulled Tom back and thrust his bag out as a shield. Wanna and Tom shrank back behind it.

The claw scratched and scrabbled around the gap in the rocks.

'It can't get us!' Tom whispered. 'Its arms are too short.'

'Maybe it will go away now,' Jamie said. But the huge unblinking eye of the T-Rex reappeared.

Wanna trembled.

'If I had a stick,' Tom muttered. 'I'd poke it in the eye!'

'There must be something we can use.' Jamie groped in his backpack. 'Let's see how it likes this.' Jamie pulled out his torch and aimed it at the T-Rex's eye. He flicked it on.

RAAAR!

The eye vanished. Cautiously, Jamie poked his head out of the crevice. The T-Rex was stomping away into the jungle.

'Whew!' Jamie said. 'I think we're safe.'

The boys gave each other a high five.

'Now, let's get out of here,' Tom said. 'Before it comes back!'

The boys and the little dinosaur climbed out of the crevice, and Wanna took the lead again, heading further downstream. 'Did you see that thing's teeth?' Jamie muttered as they splashed after their new dinosaur friend. 'That T-Rex could rip us to shreds!'

'And eat us alive, bit by bit!' Tom shuddered.

Gradually, the stream grew wider and the trees on either side began to thin out. Soon, the boys had come to the edge of the blue lagoon that they had seen earlier from Gingko Hill. Wanna stopped near a large rock and

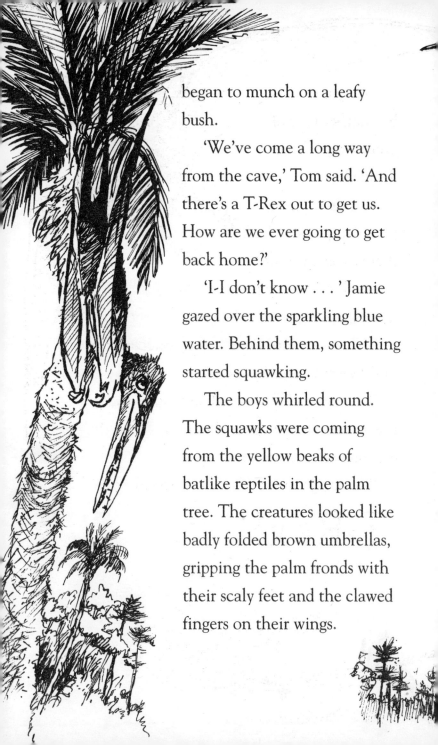

began to munch on a leafy bush.

'We've come a long way from the cave,' Tom said. 'And there's a T-Rex out to get us. How are we ever going to get back home?'

'I-I don't know . . . ' Jamie gazed over the sparkling blue water. Behind them, something started squawking.

The boys whirled round. The squawks were coming from the yellow beaks of batlike reptiles in the palm tree. The creatures looked like badly folded brown umbrellas, gripping the palm fronds with their scaly feet and the clawed fingers on their wings.

'They must be another type of pterodactyl,' Tom decided.

Just then, the pterodactyls launched themselves into the air, squawking and flapping their wings.

'What's up with them?' Tom asked as the bird-like creatures flew away.

The lagoon fell silent. The only sound was the water gently lapping the shore. Then the ground began to shake.

'Uh oh,' Jamie and Tom said together.

'T-Rex!'

CHAPTER 6

The boys turned to see the T-Rex spring out of the jungle, sending up a spray of sand. Its green scales rippled in the sunshine as it scanned the beach.

Then, it saw them.

RAAAR!

The T-Rex lowered its head. The red crests over its eyes flashed as it stomped towards them.

'We're T-Rex food,' moaned Tom.

Then, suddenly, there was a sound of
breaking branches behind them. The T-Rex's
head snapped up and it stared at the edge of
the jungle.

Turning round slowly, Jamie saw a second
T-Rex crash out of the trees onto the beach.

'Oh no!' said Tom.

It was as big as the first, but darker, with
black stripes. And it was advancing on them.

'Watch out!' Jamie rolled out of the way of a huge foot as the first T-Rex stomped to meet the other T-Rex.

Tom ducked as its tail swept over his head.

The boys watched as the first T-Rex hurled itself at the newcomer.

'They're not after us!' he breathed.

'Maybe they're fighting over territory,' Tom guessed.

The first T-Rex sank its jaws into the other's throat. The dark T-Rex screeched and writhed and thrashed its tail. Then it broke free, and sprang onto the first T-Rex's back. It hung on, biting its neck.

'Let's get out of here! Run!' Jamie dragged Tom towards the trees. Wanna bounded after them.

Gradually, the snarls and roars of the T-Rex battle faded into the jungle sounds.

'We're lost, aren't we?' Tom sat down on the ground and put his head in his hands. 'How are we going to get back?'

Grunk . . . grunk . . . grunk . . .

Wanna darted off into the trees.

'Maybe we could follow Wanna?' Jamie said. 'It's our best chance.'

After a moment, they were back at a stream. 'Is this the same stream as before?' Jamie wondered.

Next, Wanna led them down a jumble of rounded rocks.

'That's where we hid from the T-Rex!' Tom grinned.

72

They passed the purple and yellow-spotted
fungus and Jamie bent down and saw the
'W' on the tree stump. 'The Wanna tree!'
he grinned.

Then they climbed the slope through the
gingko trees and, finally, they were standing
in the mouth of the cave.

'That's how we got here!' Jamie pointed
to the fresh dinosaur footprint by the solid
rock wall.

Wanna stood next to it, and wagged his
tail. Then he stepped away, leaving two
more identical footprints, but this time
facing the rock.

'They're your footprints!'
Jamie gasped.

Wanna blinked at him, turned,
and scurried into a pile of
leaves and twigs in the
corner of the cave.

'That's Wanna's nest!' Jamie took out the last gingko fruit from his backpack.

'This is for you, Wanna,' he said, putting it on the ground. 'Thank you for helping us.' Wanna's snout poked out of his nest. He nosed the fruit back to Jamie.

'I think he wants you to have it,' Tom said.

'OK, Wanna,' said Jamie, picking it up. 'I'll put it in Dad's museum,' he told Tom, screwing up his nose and smiling.

Tom was gazing at the rock with a puzzled expression on his face. 'We stepped forward to go back in time, so maybe we have to step backwards to go forward in time,' he guessed.

Jamie nodded. 'I hope it works!'

Tom turned his back to the rock face. Then he placed his right foot in Wanna's print and stepped back with his left. There was a flash of light and Jamie found himself alone with Wanna.

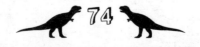

74

'It worked!' Jamie said to Wanna. 'That means we can come back and see you again!'

He patted the little dinosaur on the snout. Wanna licked Jamie's hand, then curled up in his nest.

'Goodbye, Wanna!' Jamie held the gingko fruit in one hand and his torch in the other. As he stepped back through the blaze of light, he felt the ground turn to stone beneath his feet. Then, he was back in the cave with Tom.

Jamie felt the gingko fruit in his hand soften. In the torch beam, he watched it shrivel and crumble to dust.

'We can't bring anything back,' he told Tom, letting the dust trickle between his fingers.

'It's just as well,' Tom said. 'That thing stank.'

The boys squeezed through the hole in the rock, scrambled down the boulders, and hurried down the cliff path onto the beach.

Jamie's grandad was packing up his fishing gear. He smiled at the boys as he reeled in his fishing line.

'Did you find any dinosaurs?' he asked them.

Jamie winked at Tom. 'We found a brilliant cave, didn't we, Tom?'

'Awesome!' agreed Tom. 'Let's explore it some more tomorrow!'

'Great idea!' said Jamie, hoisting up his backpack, and turning to Grandad. 'If that's OK with you and Dad?'

'Just as long as you're not getting into any scrapes . . . ' Grandad's eyes twinkled as he slung his fishing rod over his shoulder and picked up his bucket of fish.

'See you tomorrow, Tom?' Jamie said to his
new friend.

'Sure thing!' Tom said as he waved goodbye.

Jamie and Grandad walked back up the
path to the old lighthouse. Grandad asked,
'You think you'll like living round here then?'

'Definitely!' said Jamie with a grin. 'I can't
wait to explore more of Dinosaur Cove!'

DINOSAUR WORLD

- - - - BOYS' ROUTE

Jur

Misty
Lagoon

White
Ocean

 80

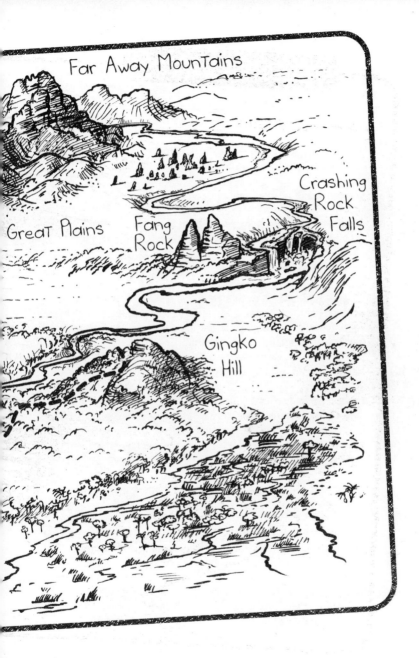

Far Away Mountains

Great Plains

Fang
Rock

Crashing
Rock
Falls

Gingko
Hill

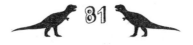

GLOSSARY

Ammonite (am-on-ite) – an extinct animal with octopus-like legs and often a spiral-shaped shell that lived in the ocean.

Conifer – cone-bearing trees such as pines or cedars.

Fossil – the remains or imprint of plants or animals found in rocks. They help scientists unravel the mysteries of prehistoric times.

Fossil Finder – hand-held computer filled with dinosaur facts.

Gingko (gink-oh) – a tree native to China called a 'living fossil' because fossils of it have been found dating back millions of years, yet they are still around today. Also known as the stink bomb tree because of its smelly apricot-like fruit.

Herbivore – an animal that only eats plants; a vegetarian.

Lagoon – a body of water, like a lake, that is separated from a larger body of water, like an ocean, by a barrier of coral or sand.

Pterodactyl (ter-oh-dak-til) – a flying prehistoric reptile which could be as small as a bird or as large as an aeroplane.

Triceratops (T-tops) (try-serra-tops) – a three-horned, plant-eating dinosaur which looks like a rhinoceros.

Tyrannosaurus Rex (T-Rex) (ti-ran-oh-sor-us rex) – a meat-eating dinosaur with a huge tail, two strong legs but two tiny arms. T-Rex was one of the biggest and scariest dinosaurs.

Wannanosaurus (wah-nan-oh-sor-us) – a dinosaur that only ate plants and used its hard, flat skull to defend itself. Named after the place it was discovered: Wannano in China.

DINOSAUR C👁VE™

CHARGE OF THE
THREE-HORNED MONSTER

by
REX STONE

illustrated by
MIKE SPOOR

Series created by
Working Partners Ltd

OXFORD
UNIVERSITY PRESS

For Jamie Heywood and Tom Vogler who have
always loved dinosaurs

Special thanks to Jan Burchett and Sara Vogler

FACT FILE

▷ JAMIE HAS JUST MOVED FROM THE CITY TO LIVE IN THE LIGHTHOUSE IN DINOSAUR COVE. JAMIE'S DAD IS OPENING A DINOSAUR MUSEUM ON THE BOTTOM FLOOR OF THE LIGHTHOUSE. WHEN JAMIE GOES HUNTING FOR FOSSILS IN THE CRUMBLING CLIFFS ON THE BEACH HE MEETS A LOCAL BOY, TOM, AND THE TWO DISCOVER AN AMAZING SECRET: A WORLD WITH REAL, LIVE DINOSAURS! BUT IT'S NOT ONLY DINOSAURS THAT INHABIT THIS PREHISTORIC WORLD...

JAMIE

- **FULL NAME:** JAMIE MORGAN
- **AGE:** 8 YEARS
- **SIZE:** 1 JATOM*
- **TOP SPEED:** 10 KPH
- **LIKES:** FOSSIL HUNTING AND LEARNING ABOUT DINOSAURS
- **DISLIKES:** BEING STUCK INDOORS

Jamie's eye

Jamie's foot

Jamie's hand

*NOTE: A JATOM IS THE SIZE OF JAMIE OR TOM: 125 CM TALL AND 27 KG IN WEIGHT

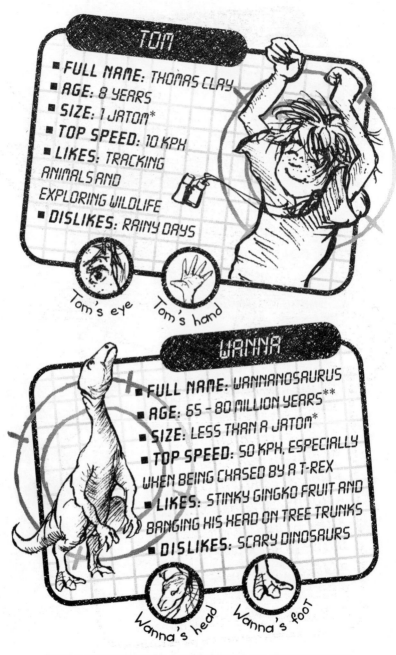

TOM

- **FULL NAME:** THOMAS CLAY
- **AGE:** 8 YEARS
- **SIZE:** 1 JATOM*
- **TOP SPEED:** 10 KPH
- **LIKES:** TRACKING ANIMALS AND EXPLORING WILDLIFE
- **DISLIKES:** RAINY DAYS

Tom's eye   Tom's hand

WANNA

- **FULL NAME:** WANNANOSAURUS
- **AGE:** 65 – 80 MILLION YEARS**
- **SIZE:** LESS THAN A JATOM*
- **TOP SPEED:** 50 KPH, ESPECIALLY WHEN BEING CHASED BY A T-REX
- **LIKES:** STINKY GINGKO FRUIT AND BANGING HIS HEAD ON TREE TRUNKS
- **DISLIKES:** SCARY DINOSAURS

Wanna's head   Wanna's foot

*NOTE: A JATOM IS THE SIZE OF JAMIE OR TOM: 125 CM TALL AND 27 KG IN WEIGHT
**NOTE: SCIENTISTS CALL THIS PERIOD THE LATE CRETACEOUS

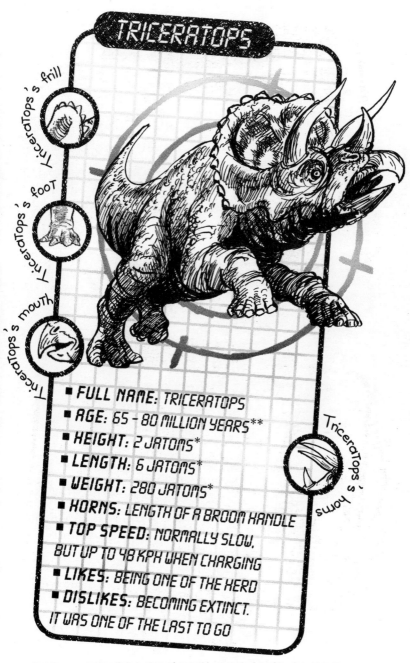

TRICERATOPS

Triceratops's frill

Triceratops's foot

Triceratops's mouth

Triceratops's horns

- **FULL NAME:** TRICERATOPS
- **AGE:** 65 – 80 MILLION YEARS**
- **HEIGHT:** 2 JATOMS*
- **LENGTH:** 6 JATOMS*
- **WEIGHT:** 280 JATOMS*
- **HORNS:** LENGTH OF A BROOM HANDLE
- **TOP SPEED:** NORMALLY SLOW. BUT UP TO 48 KPH WHEN CHARGING
- **LIKES:** BEING ONE OF THE HERD
- **DISLIKES:** BECOMING EXTINCT. IT WAS ONE OF THE LAST TO GO

*NOTE: A JATOM IS THE SIZE OF JAMIE OR TOM: 125 CM TALL AND 27 KG IN WEIGHT
**NOTE: SCIENTISTS CALL THIS PERIOD THE LATE CRETACEOUS

DINOSAUR COVE

Village

Marina

Sealight Head

Landslips where clay and fossils are

Muddy beach

DINO CAVE

Tide beach line

Sea

Smuggler's Point

Jamie Morgan sprinted along the pebbly beach of Dinosaur Cove to meet his new best friend.

'Have you got everything?' asked Tom Clay, jumping off the rock he was standing on. 'I brought my binoculars and my compass.'

Jamie took off his backpack and rummaged inside for his fossil hunting equipment. 'I've got my pocket knife, my notebook, and the Fossil Finder.' Jamie's brand new hand-held computer had all sorts of prehistoric

information at the touch of a few buttons.

'I brought some sandwiches, too,' Jamie said.
'Cheese and Grandad's home-made pickle.
It'll blow your head off!'

'I can't wait to get back to our cave,'
Tom said, hopping from one foot to another.

'You mean you can't wait to get back to
the dinosaurs!' Jamie said, as the two
friends hurried down the beach.
Jamie had met Tom for the
first time yesterday and
together they had
discovered Dinosaur
Cove's biggest secret: an
amazing world of living
dinosaurs! First, Jamie
had found a set of
fossilized dinosaur
footprints, and
then the

footprints had transported them to a place where dinosaurs still roamed the earth.

'It's hard keeping something so big a secret,' Tom confessed. 'My big brother kept asking me what I did yesterday.'

'I know!' Jamie replied. 'My dad got a huge triceratops skull fossil for the museum this morning, and I kept thinking about the *real* triceratops we saw yesterday.'

Jamie and his dad had moved in with his grandad to the old lighthouse on the cliffs and Jamie's dad planned to open a dinosaur museum on the ground floor. Jamie's dad knew more about dinosaurs than anyone, but he didn't know the colours of a T-Rex like Jamie and Tom did!

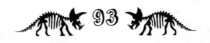

'I forgot to tell you!' panted Jamie, as they scrambled up the steep path towards their secret cave. 'I brought some coloured pencils with me. I thought we could make a map of Dino World in my notebook.'

'Good idea,' Tom said. 'We'll be like real explorers, charting unknown territories!'

'And seeing lots of dinosaurs!'

They reached the tall stack of boulders that led to their secret cave, and climbed up using cracks in the rock. From the

top of the boulders,
Jamie could see
his grandad fishing
for lobster out in
the cove.

Jamie quickly slipped
into the dark cave, but
Tom paused at the hidden
entrance. 'What if Dino
World's not there?' he asked.
'What if we dreamt it?'

Jamie laughed, and the sound echoed
around the cave. 'No way! That T-Rex we
met was definitely real!' With a shiver of
excitement he turned on his torch and shone
it into the far corner. The beam picked out
the small gap in the cave wall.

Jamie took off his backpack and crawled
through on his belly into the second chamber
which was narrower and pitch dark. Jamie

and Tom suspected they were the only people ever to have been in this place.

Jamie flashed his torch over the stone floor. 'Here are the fossilized dinosaur footprints we found yesterday.'

'The best fossil anyone has ever found!' Tom said. The footprints had somehow transported the boys to Dino World.

Tom stepped into the first clover-shaped indent in the cave floor. 'Here goes!' He placed his foot carefully into each footprint, walking in the dinosaur tracks.

Jamie stuck close behind him and counted every step. 'One . . . two . . . three . . . four . . . FIVE!'

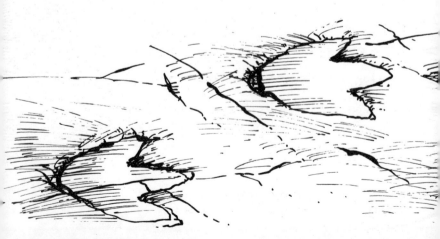

In an instant, the cold, damp cave was gone and Jamie and Tom were standing in a bright sunny cave and staring out at giant, sun-dappled trees. The air was hot and humid and they could hear the heavy drone of insects. They ran out on to the damp squelchy ground of Dino World.

'We're back in the jungle,' said Jamie happily. 'We're on Gingko Hill.'

'This is so cool!' said Tom, looking eagerly around.

Jamie laughed. 'Boiling, you mean!' He picked a large leaf off the ground and fanned himself. Suddenly he stopped. 'What was that?'

The boys listened hard. From somewhere in the steaming jungle they could hear scuffling—and it was getting nearer.

'Something's coming!' warned Tom.

Just then, a plump, scaly little creature with a flat, bony head burst out from a clump of ferns. It scuttled along on its stumpy hind legs and hurled itself at Jamie, knocking him flat on his back.

Grunk! Grunk! Grunk!

'It's Wanna!' exclaimed Tom in relief.

Jamie and Tom had met the wannanosaurus on their first visit to Dino World, and the Fossil Finder had said that it was pronounced 'wan-na-no-saur-us'. Wanna had helped them when the T-Rex was after them and turned out to be a true friend.

'Stop licking, Wanna!' panted Jamie, trying to push him off. 'Your tongue's like sandpaper.'

Tom reached up to a nearby gingko tree and picked a handful of the small, foul-smelling fruit. He held one out. 'Have a stink-o bomb, Wanna. Your favourite!'

Wanna bounded over and greedily gobbled it up as Jamie staggered to his feet. Tom gave him one more and then quickly tossed a few more pieces of the fruit to Jamie, who hid them in his backpack.

'Let's start mapping!' said Tom.

Wanna sniffed the bag as Jamie dug around and pulled out his notebook and coloured pencils. 'We're here,' he said, drawing Gingko Hill in the middle of the page. 'Yesterday we found the ocean and the lagoon in the west.' He sketched them in.

Tom checked the compass. 'So let's head north today.'

'Great,' said Jamie. 'Come on, Wanna! We're going exploring.'

Wanna wagged his tail and trotted happily alongside the boys. They scrambled through ferns and creepers and squelched among slimy giant toadstools.

At last they came to a break in the trees and peered through. Below was the dense tangle of the jungle and beyond that vast grassy plains with a wide river snaking through towards their hill.

'Look at those far away
mountains,' said Tom, scanning
the horizon with the binoculars.
'They're so high their peaks are
hidden in the clouds.'

'Far Away Mountains—that's
a good name!' said Jamie, and
scribbled it down on the map.

Then Jamie took the binoculars and
scanned the plains, and what he saw made
him gasp. There were about fifteen strange-
looking houses made of orange earth sitting
near a curve in the river.

'What is it?' Tom asked.

'I don't know,' Jamie replied. 'I think . . .
I think there's a village!'

'No way!' Tom said. He grabbed the binoculars and gasped. 'I thought we were the only people in Dino World.'

'Me too,' said Jamie. 'But . . . who could they be? There weren't any people around during dinosaur times. Humans didn't come along for millions of years!'

'Well, if *we're* here,' Tom reasoned, 'maybe other people got through too?'

'Or maybe the houses aren't for people at all, but something else,' Jamie guessed, as he

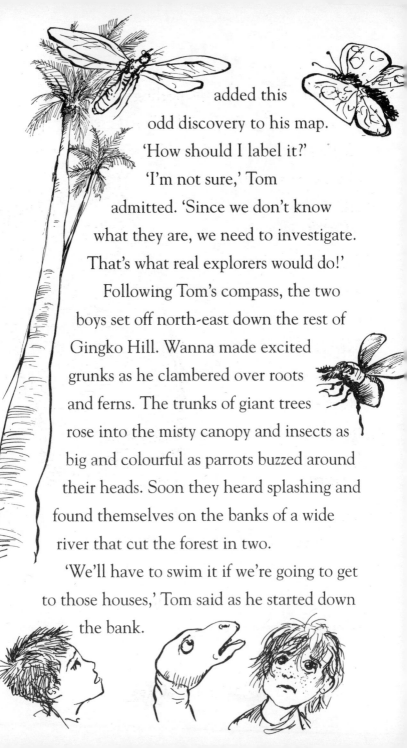

added this odd discovery to his map. 'How should I label it?'

'I'm not sure,' Tom admitted. 'Since we don't know what they are, we need to investigate. That's what real explorers would do!'

Following Tom's compass, the two boys set off north-east down the rest of Gingko Hill. Wanna made excited grunks as he clambered over roots and ferns. The trunks of giant trees rose into the misty canopy and insects as big and colourful as parrots buzzed around their heads. Soon they heard splashing and found themselves on the banks of a wide river that cut the forest in two.

'We'll have to swim it if we're going to get to those houses,' Tom said as he started down the bank.

'Wait!' warned Jamie, peeling off his backpack and pulling out his Fossil Finder. He flipped open the lid. On the screen a picture of a T-Rex footprint glowed and above it the words, **'HAPPY HUNTING'**. A cursor blinked at the bottom and Jamie tapped in the keywords: **PREHISTORIC RIVER CREATURES.**

'We might meet one of these,' he said, handing the Fossil Finder to Tom.

'CHAMPSOSAURUS,' read Tom. 'Hmm. Looks like a crocodile.'

'And we'd look like its dinner!' Jamie peered into the water for signs of life and spotted several greyish humps. 'Look over there.'

'Those
are stones, fossil-
brain,' Tom said. 'We can
cross there!'

When the three of them reached
the other side, Tom checked his
compass again and they headed off
through the trees.

'How long do you think it'll take us to get
to the houses?' Tom asked.

'Hard to tell,' puffed Jamie. 'But we've got to figure out what those things are for our map.'

The boys stumbled into a large clearing surrounded by three walls of creepers. Spiky

plants grew all over the ground, and Wanna grabbed a clump in his mouth and chomped happily.

'OK, Wanna. Lunchtime!' declared Jamie. He climbed onto a log and tore the tinfoil off the cheese and pickle sandwiches. He was just handing a sandwich to Tom when Wanna leapt up and grabbed half of it in his mouth.

'Hey, that's my lunch!' exclaimed Tom. Wanna chewed greedily. Suddenly, the little dinosaur blinked in surprise and began to run around in circles, shaking his head and making strange gak-gak noises.

'He's discovered Grandad's pickle!' Jamie laughed.

A deep rumbling sound from the forest made Jamie and Tom instantly stop laughing.

'Only something really big could make that noise,' murmured Tom, glancing over his shoulder. 'What if it's the T-Rex again?'

'Wait—I can hear mooing,' said Jamie, puzzled. His attention was fixed on the wall of creepers nearest to them.

'Like a herd of giant cows,' said Tom.

There was a sound of snapping and splitting vines. Jamie and Tom leapt to their feet as the creepers just in front of them began to shake. Jamie dropped his sandwich as the last strands tore away.

A massive beaked head with three huge horns peered into the clearing.

CHAPTER 3

SEARCH:

'It's a triceratops!' whispered Jamie, transfixed by the giant head looming above him.

'Awesome!'

Jamie and Tom could feel its hot breath on their faces. With a snort, the dinosaur forced its body through the creepers and took a lumbering step into the clearing.

'I'm glad it's not a T-Rex,' Tom said. 'But I can't believe it's so gigantic!'

'Dad was telling me about triceratops this morning,' said Jamie. 'It weighs about five

hundred and fifty kilos—the same as an elephant!'

'I don't want that treading on my toes!' Tom hastily scrambled onto the log and pulled Jamie up behind him.

The creepers shook again and another triceratops pushed its way into the clearing. Soon a whole herd of the three-horned creatures stomped into view.

One T-tops put his head down to eat some of the spiky grass right in front of them. The herd munched on the grass, completely ignoring the boys.

'Look, Wanna!' Jamie said, as their dinosaur friend gobbled up a flower nearby. 'They're herbivores, like you, which means they won't want to eat us.'

'That's true, but if one steps on us, it would be just as dangerous!' replied Tom. 'We'd better not risk trying to walk through

them. Maybe we should try to scare them
away from the clearing?'

'I don't think scaring a herd of triceratops
would be a good idea,' Jamie said. 'They

might end up charging like a herd of elephants!'

They heard a lowing from the biggest dinosaur in the herd. The sound rumbled around the clearing as the others took up the call. It shook the boys on their log.

'The leader's given a signal,' Tom said. 'What does it mean?'

'I think it means they're moving on!' said
Jamie. 'And they're going in the direction of
the houses.'

The boys tried to keep their balance as their log was bumped from all sides by the tree trunk-sized legs going by, but it was too much! Jamie slipped off the log and had to roll away quickly to avoid being trampled.

'What are we going to do?' Jamie said, breathlessly, as he scrambled safely back onto the log. 'We've got to get away from their feet!'

'It seems to me that the safest place is on top of a T-tops!' Tom said. 'Otherwise, we'll be squished!'

'Fossil-brain!' squeaked Jamie. 'We would need a trampoline to get up there.'

'Maybe we don't,' Tom said. He pulled some gingkoes out of Jamie's bag and held one out. One of the beasts stopped and sniffed the air. Then it turned its head to face the boys, and gave a blasting snort that nearly blew the boys off the log. Tom quickly dropped the gingko onto the ground. The beast lowered its gigantic head and its frill was in their reach. Its powerful jaws ground noisily as it chewed the orange fruit.

Tom tossed several other gingkoes onto the ground and whispered, 'Now, we can try to climb on board.'

Tom quickly took hold of the frill and
pulled himself onto the triceratops's forehead,
being careful not to frighten it. Then he
reached down and gave Jamie a hand up.
Soon they were both sitting on the leathery
neck and holding on to one of the
triceratops's horns.

'We're away from the huge
legs, but what if it throws us off?'
Jamie asked.

'I don't think it even
noticed us,' Tom replied.

Their triceratops finished
its gingkoes and then raised
its head and began to
follow the herd.
Wanna stared up
at them, his
head on
one side.

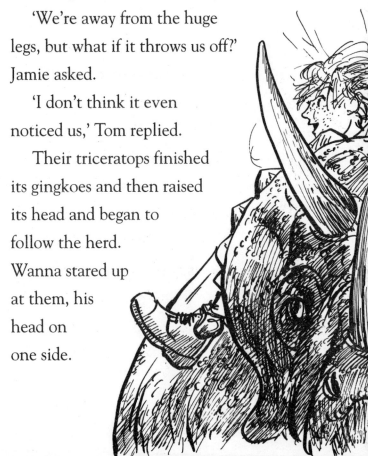

'Hey, Wanna,' waved Tom. 'Look at us!'

'This is awesome!' declared Jamie. 'It's like being on the handlebars of a giant bike.'

'Hold tight for a bumpy ride,' said Tom.

The dinosaur swayed as it plodded steadily through the tangle of jungle creepers and trees. Jamie and Tom slid about, dodging the passing branches while Wanna trotted among the legs of the herd, grunking at the top of his voice.

'This is much faster than walking!' Jamie laughed.

Suddenly the boys could see bright light through the giant leaves and branches. The herd left the jungle behind and lumbered out into the dazzling sunlight of the plains.

CHAPTER 4

Jamie squinted at the open land shimmering in the heat.

'Look!' He pointed. 'There's the river again—it comes down from the mountains.' He leaned his notebook on the triceratops's horn and drew a winding line from the mountain peaks across the plains to the jungle.

'In a way, we're the first people ever to make a map,' said Tom as the herd moved steadily across the sweltering plains.

'The first explorers, riding out on safari,' declared Jamie, laughing. 'This is great. I can see for miles!'

'Look at all these fantastic dinosaurs,' Tom said. He pointed to a slow-moving herd grazing on the leaves of some trees and spoke to an imaginary camera. 'This is Tom Clay, reporting live from Dino World, on the Great Plains. Who needs a jeep when you have the luxury of T-Tops Travel?'

Jamie laughed. He knew Tom wanted to be a famous wildlife presenter one day.

Tom went on. 'Here we are watching the alamosaurs reaching their long necks to the highest branches, and further in the distance we can see the strange dwellings that we are about to investigate. Stay tuned for what could be the most exciting discovery of all time!'

The T-tops lumbered on as the boys watched the scenery go by.

'Can you see that weird rock there?' said Tom, checking his compass. 'Over to the east.'

'It looks like a huge fang,' Jamie said. 'Let's call it Fang Rock!' He drew in the pointy rock and labelled it. Then he looked up. 'Hey, we're really close to the houses now.' He hurriedly put his notebook away. 'They're at least three times as tall as my dad!'

The thin towers stood in a silent group in the baking heat, silent and seemingly uninhabited.

'I don't think they are houses,' said Jamie. The mounds were made out of

bumpy orange dirt and had deep crevices running down them. There weren't any windows or doors, and Jamie couldn't imagine what kind of creature could live in them.

'There's no sign of any dinosaurs,' said Tom. 'This feels weird.'

'As if something's waiting to happen,' Jamie whispered.

The herd stopped a little way from the strange towers and mooed anxiously.

'They're signalling again,' said Tom. 'They don't seem to like the towers either.'

'I don't think Wanna understands their language,' Jamie said.

Instead of being cautious, Wanna was scrabbling excitedly at the bottom of one of the towers. All of a sudden, a stream of orange insects was pouring out of the hole and all over the little dinosaur.

Wanna jumped
back, batting at his face
with his claws.

'Termites!' gasped Tom.
'These are termite mounds.'

The ant-like
creatures were as big
as mice and Jamie had
never seen anything
like them.

Wanna was yelping and shaking himself as
they crawled all over him.

'Wanna is too quick for them,' said Jamie, as the little dinosaur did a frantic dance. 'He's flinging them off with all that jerking around!'

'But he's scaring the triceratops!' Tom cried.

The triceratops stamped their feet in alarm and backed off, jostling each other. The shaking of the earth seemed to wake the termites and thousands of them poured out of every mound. Jamie saw the bugs stream up the legs of the leader of the herd and into its eyes and nose.

The leader tossed its head like an angry bull to shake the insects off but it was no use. It couldn't move as easily as small, agile Wanna. Suddenly it bellowed in terror and charged straight through the termite city! Dry dirt and insects scattered everywhere.

Jamie and Tom felt their T-tops lurching forward, as the other dinosaurs began to run.

'It's a stampede!' yelled Jamie. 'Hold on!'

The boys clung to the horns as the herd took off through the cloud of orange dust. Jamie felt like a rodeo rider being bucked about. Then he felt a prickle on his leg and looked down to see a termite crawling on him. Despite the bumping, Jamie managed to flick it away quickly. But soon, a whole army of termites was crawling over their T-tops's head towards him.

Jamie tried to knock away the ones that crawled onto him, but all the movement made his backpack slip from his shoulder! He flung out an arm to catch it as it fell, but it was too late. Jamie's backpack tumbled to the ground and disappeared beneath the cloud of dust.

132

Jamie couldn't believe it. He had lost his precious Fossil Finder and his notebook and there was nothing he could do about it.

Insects were scuttling all over him now, crawling in his hair and down his neck.

'Yow!' Jamie wailed as one termite bit him on the leg. Pain shot right down to his foot, but he managed to flick another termite away.

'I've been bitten, too!' cried Tom.

The boys tried to ignore the horrible itching and just clung on for dear life.

'Where's Wanna?' yelled Tom.

'I don't know,' Jamie shouted. 'I can't see him!'

The stampede rushed forward and all at once the herd plunged downwards.

'We're going down the riverbank!' Tom leaned back and gripped tightly as they approached the water.

Jamie gulped. 'And we're not stopping!'

133

SPLASH!

Their triceratops plunged into the churning river. The boys were thrown into the water among the giant thrashing dinosaurs and drowning insects. Jamie swam up to the surface and held his hands out, keeping him away from the dinosaurs' bodies and horns.

The huge dinosaurs stood in the water, seemingly relieved that the biting termites were being swept away by the river.

'They wanted to wash the termites off,' Jamie managed to splutter.

'And us too!' Tom replied. The boys felt the pull of the river and soon were sucked into the current.

'Thanks for the ride!' Jamie called out as they left their triceratops taxi far behind.

Jamie heard a grunking noise nearby. 'Wanna!' he cried. The little dinosaur was running along the riverbank trying to keep pace with them and he had something in his mouth.

'Your backpack!' Tom exclaimed. 'It's safe!'

'Go, Wanna!' shouted Jamie.

Jamie and Tom were both good swimmers but the current was too strong to let them swim to the edge. When a log swept by, Jamie and Tom grabbed on to its stubby branches.

'Phew,' gasped Tom as he got a good hold. He checked out the river ahead. 'Do you think there are any champsosaurs in here?'

'I hope not,' Jamie groaned. 'I think we've met enough prehistoric beasts for one day.'

The boys' log floated into a patch of shadow and Tom looked up. 'It's Fang Rock!' he said. 'We must be going towards Gingko Hill—and home!'

'Maybe it will take us all the way back, and save us the walk.' Jamie grinned.

The river twisted round Fang Rock and out again into the sunshine. They could see Wanna on the bank. He was jumping up and down and grunking excitedly.

'What's the matter with Wanna?' Tom wondered aloud.

Jamie heard the sound of rushing water, and soon the boys' log was being knocked this way and that between sharp rocks. The water churned and bubbled, and Jamie realized that he could see the river ahead of them disappear. The land on either side of the river fell away and Jamie realized what Wanna was trying to warn them about. 'It's a waterfall!'

The boys kicked frantically towards the bank but the current

was too strong. The log bumped and
spun on towards the dangerous drop.

Just before the boys were about to go
over, the log caught suddenly between
two rocks. The boys only just managed
to hold on as white water crashed over
their shoulders.

'Phew!' exclaimed Jamie. He could just
see over the fall down to a large swirling
pool below and was relieved that the log
had saved them. He gave Tom a wobbly
smile. 'Let's get out of here.'

Creeeeak!

'What was that?' he gasped.

'The log's splitting from the force
of the current!' yelled Tom. 'We're going
to go over the waterfall!'

Jamie caught at his arm. 'Take a deep
breath when you fall!' he shouted urgently.
'Start swimming the moment you can!'

Crack!

The log broke and the boys were
sucked through the white foaming water
and over the edge.

'Aaaah!' Jamie shouted as he plummeted down and down.

He took a huge breath just in time.

SPLASH!

He hit the churning water and plunged under the surface, tumbling round and round. Jamie felt the waterfall pushing him to the bottom of the river. He opened his eyes but it was murky and dark and all he could see were

bubbles swirling around him. He couldn't even tell which way up was.

Then his foot touched rock. He pushed away hard, kicking his legs for all they were worth. At last he was at the surface, gulping in the wonderful air. He swam around, looking for Tom. He hoped his friend was all right!

Suddenly, the water beside him erupted and Tom bobbed up like a cork, gasping for breath.

Jamie and Tom looked up in awe at the huge waterfall they had just come over. 'We made it!'

'A huge waterfall, an army of termites, a ride on a triceratops,' Tom said. 'Another great adventure in Dino World!'

The boys swam away from the waterfall and let the gentle current take them downstream. Ahead the river disappeared

back into the jungle. The current swept them
round to the right where the trees were dense
and tangled with creepers.

The river now became wider and slower.
With weak strokes, the boys made their
way to the side and grabbed hold of an
overhanging branch.

'I can touch the bottom,' gasped Tom.
'There's a ledge.'

They dragged themselves out of the water
and collapsed on the safe, dry bank.

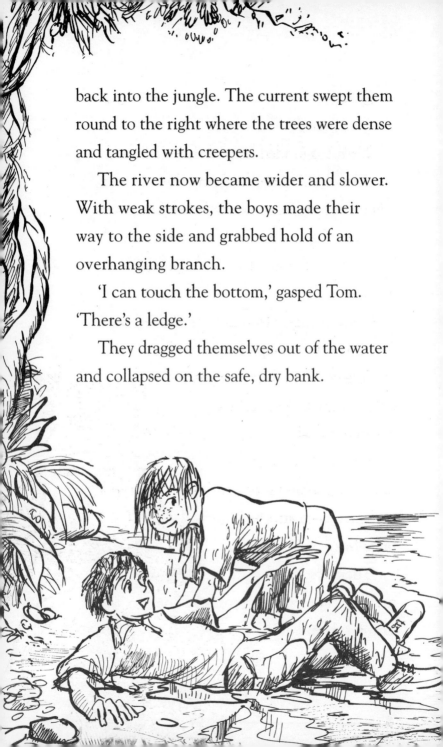

Grunk

  grunk!

Wanna bounded up and threw himself
on them, licking and nudging them in turn.
Then he disappeared into the undergrowth
and came back a moment later with the
backpack in his mouth. He dropped it in front
of the boys.

Jamie sat up. 'He kept it safe! Well done,
Wanna. You're a real mate.'

Tom reached over and got a
gingko out of the bag. 'You
deserve this!' he said, giving it
to Wanna. The little
dinosaur gobbled it down
and gave Tom another
huge lick.

'Yuck!' he cried,
pushing him away.
'Stink-o breath!'

'Where are we?' asked Jamie.

'Well, you've got the map!' laughed Tom.

Jamie pulled it out and the boys had a look around. There was a steep slope ahead of them, covered in a thick wall of trees.

'I can just hear the waterfall,' said Tom. He got to his feet and peered through the binoculars. 'Yes, it's back there. It must be— look, there's the point of Fang Rock.'

He checked his compass. 'It's east of here.'

They looked at their map.

'And the river comes from the mountains in the north-east and flows across the plains.' Jamie traced it with his finger.

'Then it goes through the jungle here— where we are,' added Tom.

Jamie gazed at the trees ahead of them. 'Then we must be at the bottom of Gingko Hill. Told you it would save us the walk!'

Tom checked his watch. 'Lucky this is waterproof,' he grinned. 'It's not long before the tide comes in. We don't want to get trapped in the cliffs.'

Jamie nodded. 'Grandad will be back with his lobsters and he'll be wondering where we are.' He picked up his backpack. 'Who'd have thought making a map would be such an adventure?'

They climbed back up Gingko Hill. As they passed the break in the trees, Jamie looked back out over the plains. He could see

the termite mounds in the distance, and
beyond that, on the other side of the river,
was the grazing triceratops herd.

'Those termite bites really hurt when we
got them,' said Jamie, pulling up his trousers to
reveal a purple pus-filled bump the size of an
apricot. 'But they don't really hurt any more.'

'Ew!' Tom crinkled up his nose. 'That
looks so gross.' Tom pulled up his
T-shirt to reveal the bite on his
stomach that had a greenish
ring around it.

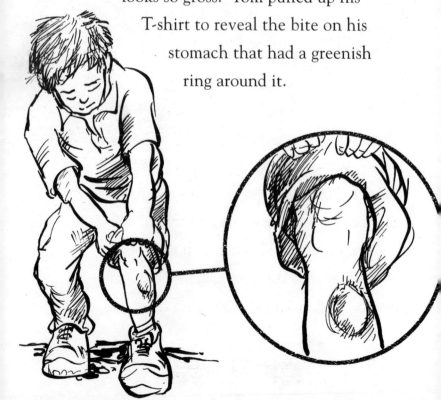

'Yours is even bigger!'
Jamie declared.

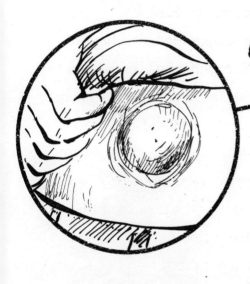

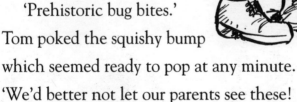

'Prehistoric bug bites.'
Tom poked the squishy bump
which seemed ready to pop at any minute.
'We'd better not let our parents see these!
We'd never be able to explain them.'

Wanna bounded along with them but
as they reached the entrance to the cave,
he slowed down and lowered his head.

Grunk?

'See you, Wanna,' said Jamie, patting him on his hard, flat head. 'We'll be back soon.'

'And that's a promise!' added Tom. He pulled out the last two gingko fruits.

Wanna wagged his tail and gobbled up his treat happily.

Jamie and Tom stepped into the cave. Jamie placed his feet in the dinosaur

footprints and felt the ground get harder as he went. On his fifth step, he was plunged into inky darkness, and he was back in the cave in Dinosaur Cove. A moment later, Tom was standing next to him.

Jamie flicked on his torch and led the way out of the cave, down the rock fall, and back along the path to the beach.

'What an adventure!' said Tom.

'Better than any theme park,' agreed Jamie. He fished out his notebook and flicked to the map. 'Look how far we travelled today! Right out on to the plains—and back the quick way!' He pointed to Fang Rock. 'The waterfall was just here. What shall we call it?'

'Crashing Rock Falls!' declared Tom.

'Cool! Maybe I'll draw us going over the edge.' Jamie grinned.

'Ahoy there, boys!' Grandad was rowing back towards the beach.

The boys waved and ran down to the sea.

'Come on,' he called. 'I can't land the boat without your help.'

Jamie and Tom jumped into the surf and waded out to the boat, helping Grandad pull the boat up the beach.

'The moment we're done, Jamie,' Grandad said as they unloaded the full lobster pots,

'you must show Tom the new triceratops skull.
It's sixty-five million years old.' He clapped
Tom on the back. 'I bet you haven't seen
anything like that before!'

Jamie and Tom smiled at each other.
Grandad would never believe what they *had*
seen today in Dino World!

DINOSAUR WORLD

- - - - - BOYS' ROUTE

Jun

Misty Lagoon

White Ocean

156

Far Away Mountains

Crashing Rock Falls

Great Plains

Fang Rock

Gingko Hill

GLOSSARY

Alamosaurus (al-am-oh-sor-us) – a gigantic dinosaur with a vegetarian diet that searched for food with its long neck and tiny head while protecting itself with its long, whip-like tail.

Champsosaurus (champ-so-sor-us) – crocodile-like prehistoric creature with a long, thin, tooth-filled snout, living and hunting in rivers and swamps.

Fossil – the remains or imprint of plants or animals found in rocks. They help scientists unravel the mysteries of prehistoric times.

Fossil Finder – hand-held computer filled with dinosaur facts.

Gingko (gink-oh) – a tree native to China called a 'living fossil' because fossils of it have been found dating back millions of years, yet they are still around today. Also known as the stink-bomb tree because of its smelly apricot-like fruit.

Herbivore – an animal that only eats plants; a vegetarian.

Termite – ant-like insects that grow as big as mice in Dino World. These prehistoric pests lived and worked together to build orange house-high mounds out of soil and spit, and there are still several kinds of termites around today.

Triceratops (T-tops) (try-serra-tops) – a three-horned, plant-eating dinosaur which looks like a rhinoceros.

Tyrannosaurus Rex (T-Rex) (ti-ran-oh-sor-us rex) – a meat-eating dinosaur with a huge tail, two strong legs but two tiny arms. T-Rex was one of the biggest and scariest dinosaurs.

Wannanosaurus (wah-nan-oh-sor-us) – a dinosaur that only ate plants and used its hard, flat skull to defend itself. Named after the place it was discovered: Wannano in China.

DINOSAUR COVE™

MARCH OF THE ARMOURED BEASTS

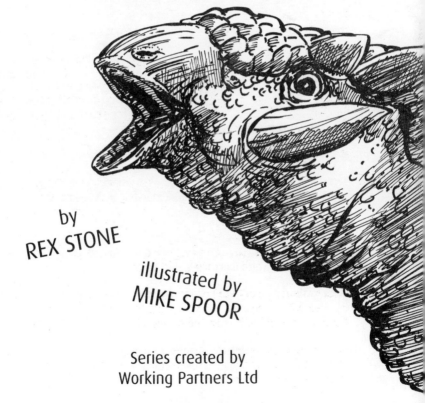

by
REX STONE

illustrated by
MIKE SPOOR

Series created by
Working Partners Ltd

OXFORD
UNIVERSITY PRESS

With special thanks to Jane Clarke

To all my SCBWI friends

FACT FILE

▷ JAMIE HAS JUST MOVED FROM THE CITY TO LIVE IN THE LIGHTHOUSE IN DINOSAUR COVE. JAMIE'S DAD IS OPENING A DINOSAUR MUSEUM ON THE BOTTOM FLOOR OF THE LIGHTHOUSE. WHEN JAMIE GOES HUNTING FOR FOSSILS HE MEETS A LOCAL BOY, TOM, AND THE TWO DISCOVER A WORLD WITH REAL LIVE DINOSAURS! TRACKING DINOSAURS IS EXCITING, BUT DANGER SURROUNDS THE BOYS AT EVERY TURN.

JAMIE

- **FULL NAME:** JAMIE MORGAN
- **AGE:** 8 YEARS
- **SIZE:** 1 JATOM*
- **TOP SPEED:** 10 KPH
- **LIKES:** FOSSIL HUNTING AND LEARNING ABOUT DINOSAURS
- **DISLIKES:** BEING STUCK INDOORS

Jamie's eye

Jamie's foot

Jamie's hand

*NOTE: A JATOM IS THE SIZE OF JAMIE OR TOM: 125 CM TALL AND 27 KG IN WEIGHT

TOM

- **FULL NAME:** THOMAS CLAY
- **AGE:** 8 YEARS
- **SIZE:** 1 JATOM*
- **TOP SPEED:** 10 KPH
- **LIKES:** TRACKING ANIMALS AND EXPLORING WILDLIFE
- **DISLIKES:** RAINY DAYS

Tom's eye Tom's hand

WANNA

- **FULL NAME:** WANNANOSAURUS
- **AGE:** 65 – 80 MILLION YEARS**
- **SIZE:** LESS THAN A JATOM*
- **TOP SPEED:** 50 KPH, ESPECIALLY WHEN BEING CHASED BY A T-REX
- **LIKES:** STINKY GINGKO FRUIT AND BANGING HIS HEAD ON TREE TRUNKS
- **DISLIKES:** SCARY DINOSAURS

Wanna's head Wanna's foot

*NOTE: A JATOM IS THE SIZE OF JAMIE OR TOM: 125 CM TALL AND 27 KG IN WEIGHT
**NOTE: SCIENTISTS CALL THIS PERIOD THE LATE CRETACEOUS

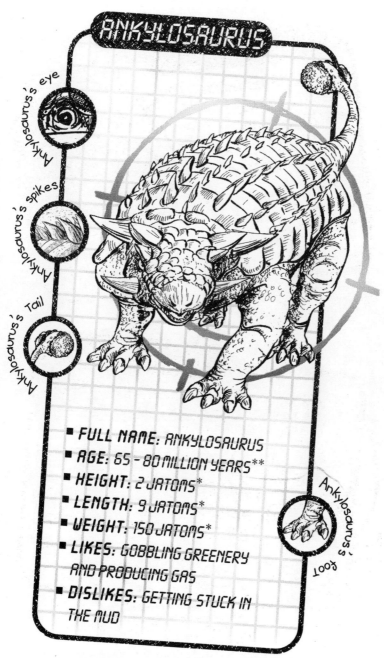

ANKYLOSAURUS

Ankylosaurus's eye

Ankylosaurus's spikes

Ankylosaurus's Tail

Ankylosaurus's foot

- **FULL NAME:** ANKYLOSAURUS
- **AGE:** 65 - 80 MILLION YEARS**
- **HEIGHT:** 2 JATOMS*
- **LENGTH:** 9 JATOMS*
- **WEIGHT:** 150 JATOMS*
- **LIKES:** GOBBLING GREENERY AND PRODUCING GAS
- **DISLIKES:** GETTING STUCK IN THE MUD

*NOTE: A JATOM IS THE SIZE OF JAMIE OR TOM: 125 CM TALL AND 27 KG IN WEIGHT
**NOTE: SCIENTISTS CALL THIS PERIOD THE LATE CRETACEOUS

DINOSAUR COVE

Village

Marina

Sealight Head

CHAPTER 1

Jamie picked out a small fossil from the heap of gooey mud that had slipped down onto Dinosaur Cove beach in the night. The stone looked like a stubby pencil with a sharp point. He wiped it on his jeans and handed it to his best friend Tom.

'That could be a dinosaur tooth,' Jamie's grandad said, putting down his fishing bucket and leaning in for a closer look.

'It's not a dinosaur tooth,' Tom replied. 'They don't look anything like this in real li—'

Jamie nudged
Tom with his elbow.
Grandad didn't
know they'd
discovered real live
dinosaurs through a secret cave
in Dinosaur Cove.

'Let's find out what it is.' Jamie rummaged
inside his backpack. 'Compass . . . cheese and
pickle sandwiches . . . Fossil Finder!' Jamie
flipped open the lid of the hand-held
computer and typed 'stubby pencil' in the
search box. At once a picture of the fossil
popped up.

'*BEL-EM-NITE*,' he read. '*THIS BULLET-SHAPED
FOSSIL IS THE BODY OF A SEA CREATURE LIKE A SQUID.*'
Jamie snapped the Fossil Finder shut and put
it, and the belemnite, in his backpack.

'Fossil squid, eh?' Grandad chuckled. 'You
can't eat those! I'm off to find some *fresh* fish.'

'And we should go find some fresh dinosaurs,' Tom whispered to Jamie as Grandad gathered up his fishing gear.

'Don't get stuck in the mud!' Grandad's eyes twinkled as he turned towards the sea. 'It'll swallow you up and spit out your bones, just like it did to the dinosaurs . . .'

The instant Grandad was out of hearing range, the boys yelled, 'Dino World here we come!'

They dashed towards the path that led from the beach up to the smugglers' cave where the hidden entrance to Dino World was. At the bottom of the path, Jamie spotted two large footprints in the sand.

Jamie skidded to a halt. 'Wait, Tom. Someone has been here!'

Tom bent down to examine the shoe imprints. 'They're fresh,' he said, 'and they're leading up our path!'

'Oh no,' Jamie groaned. 'What if someone's found the way through our cave into Dino World?'

'Then it wouldn't be our secret any more,' Tom said grimly. 'You know grown-ups. They'd sell tickets to visitors to make money out of it.'

Jamie frowned. 'Or they'd say it was dangerous and close

it up completely. We might never get to go back!'

Jamie and Tom examined the ground carefully and followed the footprints up the steep slope to the pile of boulders beneath their secret cave.

'Someone definitely came this way,' Jamie said.

'We've got to make sure the cave's safe.' He clambered up the boulders as fast as he could.

'What are you waiting for?' he called from the top. Tom was lingering over a footprint beneath the boulders. Jamie hopped impatiently from one foot to another as Tom scaled the boulders and hauled himself up next to Jamie.

'There's no need to panic.' Tom grinned and led the way into the cool cave. 'No one came in here. Those footprints went on past the boulders. Our cave is safe!'

'But what if they come back?' Jamie flicked on his torch and shone it into the corner of the cave. The light disappeared into the gap they'd discovered on their first visit.

'Stop worrying,' Tom told him. 'There's no way someone with feet that big could get through here.'

'You're right.' Jamie breathed a sigh of relief as he pushed his backpack through the tiny gap and crawled in after it, followed closely by Tom.

He flashed his torch over the floor of the secret chamber and picked out the fossilized footprints

of their dinosaur friend,
Wanna, which had led
them twice into Dino World.

'That foot wouldn't fit in these
tracks, either.' Jamie stepped into the first
of the small clover-shaped prints in the solid
rock. 'But they're exactly the right size for us!'

'Then let's track dinosaurs!' Tom declared.
'I'm right behind you.'

'One . . . two . . . three . . . ' Jamie's heart
beat faster as he counted each step. *What kind
of dinosaurs will we see today?* he wondered.

' . . . four . . . '

The cave wall in front of him looked like
solid rock, but as he put his foot forward a
crack of light appeared.

'FIVE!'

The crack of light widened and the ground
felt soft under Jamie's trainers as he stepped
from the dark cave into Dino World.

Jamie stood blinking in the sunlight as the familiar smells of wet leaves and stinky gingko fruit filled his nose. A moment later, Tom was standing next to him on Gingko Hill.

'Wanna! Here, Wanna!' Jamie raised his voice above the buzzing insects and the calls of creatures in the steamy jungle.

'That's strange,' Tom said. 'He usually comes right away.'

'Maybe we could track him,' Jamie wondered aloud.

Jamie and Tom examined the ground outside the cave for traces of their faithful dinosaur friend and saw fresh footprints—just like the fossilized ones back in the cave— leading down the side of Gingko Hill.

'Wanna's gone south, down the hill,' Tom said, looking at his compass. 'We've never been that way before. Let's follow him!'

'Hang on a minute.' Jamie picked some smelly gingko fruit and put them in his backpack. 'For Wanna when we see him.'

Then the boys hurried down the hill.

'This is steep!' Jamie said as his legs picked up speed.

'Beat you to the bottom!' Tom yelled.

Jamie raced his friend down the hill, skidding and sliding, grabbing at trailing vines and low branches to keep from falling head over heels.

Jamie leaped down the last little way to land in the soft mud at the base of the hill.

Splat!

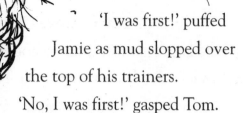

'I was first!' puffed Jamie as mud slopped over the top of his trainers.

'No, I was first!' gasped Tom.

A glob of mud plopped off his curly red hair and splattered onto his freckly nose.

They looked at each other and laughed.

'Shh!' said Tom. 'I can hear a squishing noise.'

Jamie listened for a moment and then whirled round as a wet, sandpapery tongue licked his cheek.

'Yuck!' he yelled.

'It's Wanna!' Tom cheered.

The little green and brown dinosaur wagged his tail, splattering mud all over them. Then he cocked his bony head to one side and looked hopefully at Jamie's backpack.

'Here you are, Wanna.' Jamie handed Wanna a stinky gingko fruit.

The little dinosaur grunked happily as he
gobbled up the fruit, then he bounded up
to Tom.

'Urgh, stinko breath! Aargh!' Tom landed
on his back in the mud with Wanna on top of
him, licking his face.

The mud squelched as Tom wrestled with
Wanna. Jamie looked at the ground more

closely. It was churned up and rutted as far as he could see.

'Stop mucking about!' he told Tom. 'We're standing in the middle of a dinosaur trackway.'

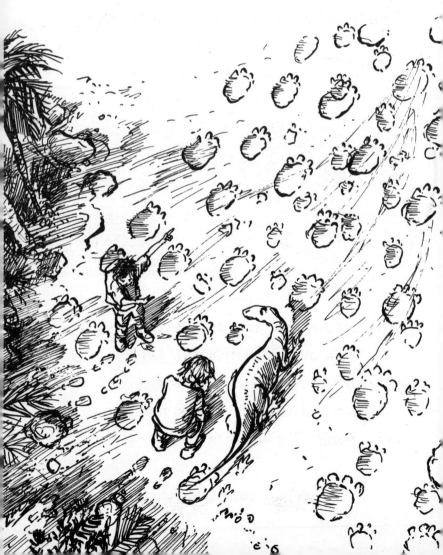

'What do you mean?' Tom asked, disentangling himself from Wanna.

'Look at all these footprints. A group of big, heavy dinosaurs have made this path.' Jamie pointed to a clear footprint at the edge of the track. He stepped on the mud next to it. The dinosaur footprint was over twice as long and much, much deeper than his. Jamie and Tom bent down and looked carefully at the print. There were four bumps for toes at the front.

'They're all heading that way.' Jamie pointed the way the toes were facing.

Tom wiped his muddy face with the sleeve of his T-shirt. 'Let's track them!'

'Definitely,' agreed Jamie.

They trudged off along the muddy trackway with Wanna squishing along beside them. Suddenly, Wanna froze, his tail sticking out straight behind him.

The boys stopped and listened. For a moment there was silence, and then strange dinosaur calls began to boom down the trackway.

Aroop! Aroop! Aroooop!

'They sound like foghorns!' Jamie shuddered as the creepy calls echoed around them. Chills were running up and down his spine.

'Are we sure we want to catch up with those dinosaurs?' Tom asked nervously. 'What if they're meat eaters?'

'Good point.' Jamie wiped his muddy hands on his T-shirt, and took the Fossil Finder out of his backpack. He flipped it open and tapped in: DINOSAUR TRACKS, FOUR TOES.

'FOSSIL FOOTPRINTS ARE RARER THAN FOSSIL BONES,' he read. 'ROUNDED FOOTPRINTS WITH FOUR TOE MARKS AT THE FRONT WERE MADE BY HEAVY PLANT EATERS.'

Tom beamed. 'Dinosaurs here we come!'

CHAPTER 3

SEARCH:

As Jamie, Tom, and Wanna followed the trackway, the trees began to thin out and the ground got wetter. Jamie's footsteps sank deeper and deeper into the mud and a thin fog drifted around them.

Even though they'd left the jungle behind, the tracks stayed at the same width. 'These dinosaurs are walking in a line,' Tom realized.

'Like elephants in those wildlife documentaries.' Jamie said, as he leapt over a giant purple and orange mushroom.

'How many are there?'
Tom asked.

'I can't tell,' Jamie said,
as his sodden jeans flapped
around his legs. 'They've
stomped all over each
other's tracks. Maybe a
T-Rex was chasing them?'

'I don't think so,' Tom
said. 'If they were running,
we'd see their toes digging
into the ground. They're
on a steady march.'

'Like an army!' Jamie
said, pausing beneath a
tree with moss dripping
from its twisted branches.
He peered through the
thickening mist. A fresh,
salty, tangy smell filled the

foggy air. Wanna took a
deep sniff and sneezed.

'This must be a marsh where
the river widens out and joins the ocean,'
Tom said.

Jamie narrowed his eyes. Strange
shapes were moving through the murk
like ghosts. Dinosaur calls echoed
across the marshland.

'Spooky!' Jamie shuddered.

'It's OK. They're plant eaters,
remember?' Tom squelched off into the mist,
followed by Wanna. Jamie watched as their

footprints filled up with
bright green slime
the instant they'd made
them. He bent down and
looked more carefully at
the sludgy tracks. A series
of puddle footprints that

looked like smaller versions of the dinosaur prints they were tracking branched off from the path. He followed them as they zigzagged through the marsh.

'Hey, Tom!' he called.

Tom didn't reply. Jamie peered through the fog. He listened, but all he could hear were

the swarms of insects and the plopping and gurgling of the marsh.

'Tom?' he yelled. 'Wanna?'

Jamie swallowed hard; he was all alone.

At last he heard a familiar noise.

Grunk, grunk!

'Wanna!' Jamie breathed a sigh of relief.

Wanna bounded out of the mist and licked Jamie's cheek. Tom splashed after him.

'Wanna sniffed you out,' he explained. 'I thought you were tracking the herd behind me.'

'I was following these baby tracks,' Jamie said, pointing them out to Tom. 'It must have wandered off on its own.'

'Babies should stay close to the adults for protection.' Tom frowned. 'That baby could be easy pickings for a predator. We should help it get back to its herd!'

'In this fog?' Jamie asked. As he spoke, he felt a breeze on his face and the fog tumbled

across the marsh, lifting a little. Wanna
snuffled happily around the slime pools
towards a plant with rubbery-looking leaves
and bright yellow flowers the size of dinner
plates.

'The bog doesn't worry Wanna,' Tom said.
'We'll be OK if we're careful.'

They watched as Wanna grabbed a flower
in his mouth, pulled it off and chewed it up.

Then he bounded back to the boys with his nose covered in yellow pollen.

'Tasty?' Jamie asked him.

Wanna wagged his tail.

'Perhaps those flowers tempted the baby away from the herd,' Tom said.

'Let's try and find him,' Jamie said and picked his way across the marsh following the baby footprints, trying to avoid the bright green sludge.

'It definitely came this way.' Tom pointed to a torn up patch of flowers.

As Jamie looked up, he tripped on a rock half-buried in the mud and staggered forwards, sinking up to his shins in a pool of green sludge.

'Urgh! This mud stinks of rotten eggs.' Jamie tried to step back onto the firmer ground, but his feet wouldn't move.

Bluurp!

The slime bubbled up to his knees.

'Uh oh,' Jamie said, struggling to move.

'I'm sinking into the bog!'

CHAPTER 4

Jamie tried again to pull his legs free from the bog, but it didn't help. Now, the mud was up to his thighs.

'Stop moving!' Tom yelled. 'You'll sink even quicker if you thrash around. You've got to lie down!'

Jamie looked down at the liquid mud swirling around his legs. 'You're joking.'

'You have to spread out your body weight,' Tom said urgently. 'It's the only way to get yourself out!'

Jamie took a deep breath and then threw himself flat in the revolting green goo. Slime oozed into his mouth, ears, and nose, but at least he stopped sinking. 'It's working!' he spluttered as he crawled out onto the firm ground by the marsh plant and stood dripping.

'This place is dangerous!' he told Tom. 'We should go back.'

'We can't go back, yet,' Tom said. 'Listen!'

Jamie scooped out the slime from his ears. Now he could hear a pitiful wailing echoing across the bog.

Aooo, aooo, aooo!

It was coming from behind a curtain of creepers that hung from the branches of a stunted tree. Jamie and Tom walked carefully towards the sound, jumping over the bright green patches of sinking slime. At the stunted tree, Wanna stopped to munch on another patch of yellow marsh plants.

The boys parted the creepers and saw a
dinosaur the size of a small car up to its belly in
the sludge. It was covered in thick bony plates
from the tip of its beaky nose to the enormous
club at the end of its tail. Two rows of spikes ran
down its wide body and large horns stuck out
from the back of its head. It looked at them
mournfully and opened its mouth.

Aoo-ooo, it wailed, thrashing its club
against the trunk of the tree. Splinters of
rotten wood splattered into the marsh.

'What is it?' Tom asked.

Jamie was already tapping words '*BONY PLATES, SPIKED TAIL*' into the Fossil Finder.

'*AN-KY-LO-SAUR-US,*' he read.

'*AN ARMOURED DINOSAUR AS STRONG AS A TANK. THIS SMALL-BRAINED DINOSAUR ATE TOUGH PLANTS AND PROBABLY PRODUCED GREAT QUANTITIES OF GASEOUS WASTE.*'

Jamie snapped the Fossil Finder shut and returned it to his backpack. He looked at the baby dinosaur.

'This anky is small-brained, all right. The more it thrashes its tail, the faster it sinks in the mud!'

'A bit like you, then!' Tom grinned.

Jamie threw a glob of mud at him.

Aooo-oooo! the baby wailed. Wanna started to grunk in sympathy. The anky thumped its tail against the stinky sludge.

'How are we going to get it out?' Jamie sighed.

'We'll have to calm it down first,' Tom said. 'But how do you calm down a dinosaur?'

Jamie looked at Wanna, whose nose was still plastered in pollen. 'Feed it!'

Jamie took a handful of gingko fruit out of his backpack and tossed them, one by one, towards the baby anky. Wanna rushed in and gobbled them up as fast as Jamie could throw them. Then he dashed back to Jamie and stood dribbling and wagging his tail.

'We'll have to try something you don't like!' Jamie rummaged in his backpack and unwrapped the cheese and pickle sandwiches Grandad had made for their lunch.

Wanna sneezed and backed off, shaking his head and making *gak-gak* noises.

Jamie threw a sandwich under the baby anky's beak. It stopped thrashing its tail and sniffed suspiciously at it. Then it started to squeal as if it was being poisoned and began thrashing its tail again.

'Ankys don't like your grandad's pickle, either!' Tom said. 'What else can we try?'

'The marsh plant!' Jamie turned back to the marsh plants and wrenched off three large yellow flower heads. 'One for you, Wanna!'

Wanna pounced on it in delight.

Jamie skimmed the other two across the marsh like a frisbee. The baby dinosaur's long tongue flickered out and pulled a yellow flower into its mouth.

As it chewed, the anky's tail stopped thrashing.

'It's working! Let's get some more flowers.' Jamie bent to pick some more.

'Wait!' Tom said. 'Listen.'

A deep, mournful bellowing was coming from the other side of the tree.

Aroo! Aroo! Aroooo!

Jamie and Tom whirled round. An enormous beaky head loomed out of the mist. The baby began squeaking excitedly.

'That must be the baby's mother,' Tom said.

The huge ankylosaurus lumbered slowly towards them.

'Awesome!' Jamie gasped. 'She's as big as a tank. And look at the size of that club at the end of her tail!'

The mum anky stopped. She stared at Jamie, Tom, and Wanna. Then she began to beat her clubbed tail into the marsh, sending up plumes of muddy spray.

'Uh oh,' Jamie whispered. 'She doesn't like us.'

Aroooomph! she snorted.

Wanna tried to hide behind Jamie.

'She's going to charge us!' Tom yelled.

'Run!'

CHAPTER 5

SEARCH:

The boys and Wanna darted behind the twisted tree trunk.

'What's happening?' Tom asked.

Jamie peered out.

'She's not charging! She must know she'll get stuck if she comes any closer.' He looked over to the baby anky. It had stopped squealing and thumping its tail.

Maybe there is still a chance to help it, Jamie thought.

Tom crept out from the cover of the tree.

205

'The poor thing's stopped thrashing,' he said. 'It's exhausted!'

'We can get close to it now,' Jamie said. 'Perhaps we can push it out.'

'It's worth a try,' Tom agreed. 'As long as the mum will let us.'

The boys picked their way round to the back of the baby.

'OK,' said Jamie. 'The ground's solid here.

Be careful not to step into the slime and watch
out for that tail! One, two, three . . .
heave!'

They pushed as hard as they could, but the
baby dinosaur didn't budge.

Beneath the anky's armoured bottom, the
swamp began to gloop and burble. There was
a loud whooshing noise and the surface of the
slime boiled.

Plop! Plop! Plop!

The bubbles burst, splattering their faces
with gunge.

A hideous smell welled up around them.
Jamie coughed and gagged. It was even worse
than rotten eggs.

'What's that smell?' Tom gurgled. His face
was dripping with green slime.

'Anky gas!' Jamie gagged. 'It farted!'

'I didn't know baby ankys had rocket boosters,' Tom gasped, fanning at the air.

'They'd be easier to get out of the bog if they did.' Jamie grimaced. 'One more try!'

The baby anky didn't move.

'It's like trying to push a truck,' Jamie groaned.

'That's what we need,' said Tom. 'A truck to pull it out of the swamp.'

'Or a tank . . . ' Jamie looked across at the mum ankylosaurus and thought hard. 'We might not have a truck or a tank,' he said, 'but we do have the next best thing.'

Tom grinned. 'You're right! Now all we need is some rope.'

The boys looked at each other.

'Creepers!' they yelled together, rushing back to the tree where Wanna was munching on marsh plants. He wagged his tail as they came up to him.

'No time to play,' Jamie told him. 'We're busy!'

Jamie and Tom heaved at the dangling creepers, but they didn't break off.

'It's good that they're strong,' Tom said. 'But we've got to get some down!'

'I'll climb up and cut some off.' Jamie shinned up a vine, straddled the branch and rummaged in his backpack, pulling out the fossil belemnite. 'I knew this would come in useful,' he muttered and used the fossil's sharp point to hack away at the vines.

As the creepers fell to the ground, Jamie swung back down to Tom.

Fig 1

'We'll need to tie them together,' he told Tom. 'Do you know any good knots?'

Tom nodded. 'A fisherman's knot!' Tom showed Jamie how to do it.

Fig 2

Soon, they had three long lengths of vine. They twisted them together for strength, and made a big loop at each end.

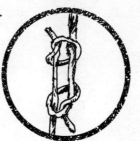

Fig 3

'We'll need some treats,' Tom said. Wanna watched hopefully as the boys stuffed their pockets with the yellow marsh plant petals.

'Not for you,' Jamie told him. 'For the ankys.'

Fig 4

Fisherman's knot

Wanna seemed a little disappointed.

'Now we've got to get these loops around the dinosaurs,' Jamie told Tom. The boys sloshed back to the baby anky and Tom dropped a flower for him to eat. Then Tom carefully threw his loop over the baby's head.

'That's the easy bit.' Jamie clutched the loop at the other end of the vines. 'Now for the mum . . . ' He pulled a handful of petals from his pocket and slowly approached her.

The mum anky fixed Jamie with her hooded eyes and lowered her head. Her tail beat the sludge, splattering him with stagnant water. Jamie threw a petal in front of her. She sniffed at it and ate it.

'So far, so good,' Jamie murmured. He crept closer and threw a whole handful of petals to the side. She twisted round to eat them.

 213

'Watch out!' Tom yelled.

Jamie jumped out of the way as the club on the end of the mum's tail whipped past his head.

'Throw more flowers!' Tom called. 'Turn her right round.'

Jamie flung more petals on the marsh, moving around to keep out of the way of the clubbed tail. The mum anky turned and began to graze. Jamie picked up the vine rope and took hold of the loop.

He threw it, like a lasso, over her shoulders, but it snagged on one of the horns.

'Missed!' Jamie muttered. The anky carried on chewing peacefully on the petals.

'She hasn't noticed,'
Tom called.

'I'll unhook it and try again!'

Jamie crept towards her and took hold of
the loop wedged behind her horn. He could feel
the steam from her nostrils as he worked it free.

Suddenly the baby anky began to snort
and wail.

Aroooph! The mum anky lifted her
head, jerking Jamie off his feet. His wrist was
caught in the vines!

Aroop, aroop, aroop!

The mum anky stumbled into the bog, with
Jamie dangling from her neck. He struggled to
get loose as her tail thrashed angrily, but he was
stuck. Then the two front legs of the huge beast
began to sink into the pool of sludge.

I'm doomed, Jamie thought. *Like Grandad said,
the mud will swallow me up and spit out my bones!*

CHAPTER 6

Dangling just above the slime, Jamie realized that the safest place to be was on top of the dinosaur.

Pulling with all his might, he hauled himself up onto the back of the mum anky's neck. He untangled the loop from the horn, then quickly reached down over her head and slipped it around her neck.

Tom was gawping at him.

Jamie gave Tom the thumbs up sign and got unsteadily to his feet. His muddy trainers

got a grip on the anky's
rough plating and he turned
and ran along the anky's
thick neck and up over her
wide body between the two
rows of spikes. He sprang
off her back and landed
next to Tom.

'Awesome!' Tom
grinned. 'You just ran
over a dinosaur!'

'Better than a dinosaur running over me,'
Jamie said. 'Now all we've got to do is turn
her round again and get her to pull her baby
out. We'll need lots of petals for that!'

The boys gathered armfuls of the juiciest
looking marsh plants.

'Here, Anky!'
Jamie threw some
plants just out of reach
of the mum ankylosaurus.

The great beast lifted her
front legs out of the sludge,
moved slowly towards them and
began to chew.

'More!' Tom threw more petals in front
of her. As the mum strained towards them,
the length of vine attaching her to her baby
tightened.

'It's working!' Tom cheered as the mum
anky lurched forward onto dry land heaving
her baby out after her. The baby struggled to
its feet.

'Yes!' Jamie and Tom
leaped into the air to give
each other a high five as the
mum anky turned and touched
beaks with her baby.
'We'd better take off the vines,'
Jamie said.

'My turn!' Tom grinned. 'You keep them busy eating.'

Wanna bounded up, wagging his tail. He dropped a mouthful of petals at Jamie's feet.

'Thanks, Wanna, that's just what we need.' Jamie threw petals in front of the ankys' beaks. As they munched, Tom carefully unhitched the vines from their necks and slowly backed away.

The ankys stopped eating. They raised their heads together and made a soft high-pitched oooping noise.

'I think they're saying thank you!' Jamie said in amazement.

As Jamie, Tom, and Wanna watched, the mist thinned. The mum gently nudged her baby and they turned away from the boys. Ahead of them, a line of ankylosaurs was marching slowly onwards.

'It's the rest of their herd!' As Jamie spoke,
the mum and baby lumbered over to the line
calling *Aroop!*

The herd stopped and turned their heads.
Arooo! Aroo! They lowed in reply as mum
and baby caught up with them. The mum
nudged her baby between the legs of the
biggest ankylosaurus.

'That must be the dad,' Tom said.

The mum anky moved in behind him as the herd of armoured beasts continued its march.

Wanna grunked happily and turned back towards the trackway.

'Our first dino rescue,' Jamie said with satisfaction. 'But Wanna's right. It's time to go home.'

'You should see yourself!' Tom laughed as they trudged after Wanna. 'You're a sight!'

'Look who's talking!' Jamie grinned. Tom was covered from head to toe in stinky green marsh mud.

They trekked up Gingko Hill and stopped by Wanna's nest.

'We have to go back now, Wanna,' Jamie told him. He took the last of the gingko fruit out of his backpack.

Grunk grunk. Wanna wagged his tail and settled down happily to chew his treat.

'See you next time!'

Jamie stepped backwards through the dinosaur footprints, feeling the ground turn to stone under his feet. He was back in the cave, and a moment later Tom stood beside him.

Jamie shone his torch on Tom. The green slime that had covered him in Dino World had turned into a thick layer of dust.

 228

He sniffed at the dust on his own T-shirt.

'Yuck!' he sneezed. 'It still stinks of marsh and anky gas. We'd better get it off before anyone notices.'

They squeezed back through the gap and scrambled down the boulders towards the beach. The tide was out. In the distance, Grandad waved and began to pick up his fishing gear. Jamie waved back.

'Beat you into the sea!' he challenged Tom.

The boys raced across the beach, threw themselves into the sea, and came up spluttering.

'I was first,' laughed Jamie.

'No, I was first,' grinned Tom.

They splashed water all over each other until they were sure they'd washed off every trace of ankylosaurus.

'Ahoy there, me hearties,' Grandad greeted them as they emerged dripping from the sea. 'It looks as if you've had fun today!'

'Great fun!' Tom said. 'But I'd better be getting home now. See you tomorrow, Jamie?'

'You bet!' Jamie waved as Tom set off for the village.

'What have you boys been up to?' Grandad asked Jamie as they walked up towards the lighthouse.

'We've been tracking dinosaurs!' Jamie told him. 'But don't worry, Grandad— we were careful. We didn't get stuck in the mud.'

DINOSAUR WORLD

----- BOYS' ROUTE

Jur

Misty
Lagoon

White
Ocean

Far Away Mountains

Great Plains

Fang
Rock

Crashing
Rock
Falls

Gingko
Hill

GLOSSARY

Ankylosaurus (an-ki-low-sor-us) – a vegetarian dinosaur known for its armoured coat and clubbed tail (see below). Its armour consisted of large bony bumps similar to the covering of modern-day crocodiles and lizards.

Belemnite (bell-em-nite) – an extinct squid-like sea creature. Belemnite had ten arms of similar length with small hooks and beak-like mouths. Its fossils usually only preserve the creature's bullet-shaped body.

Bog – wetlands with soggy, spongy ground that are often too soft to walk across.

Clubbed tail – the tail of an ankylosaurus which resembled a huge, armoured golf club. The ankylosaurus used its tail as a weapon and could break bones of its enemies with a swift swing.

Fisherman's knot – named for its usefulness to fishermen. Two knots are tied in two ropes lying side by side. Tie a knot in one rope and slip the other rope through the hole; then tighten. Do the same to the other rope.

Fossil Finder – hand-held computer filled with dinosaur facts.

Gingko (gink-oh) – a tree native to China called a 'living fossil' because fossils of it have been found dating back millions of years, yet they are still around today. Also known as the stink bomb tree because of its smelly apricot-like fruit.

Marsh – shallow wetlands that are almost continuously flooded by a variety of sources, including rain, streams, and the sea.

Predator – an animal that hunts and eats other animals.

Wannanosaurus (wah-nan-oh-sor-us) – a dinosaur that only ate plants and used its hard, flat skull to defend itself. Named after the place it was discovered: Wannano in China.

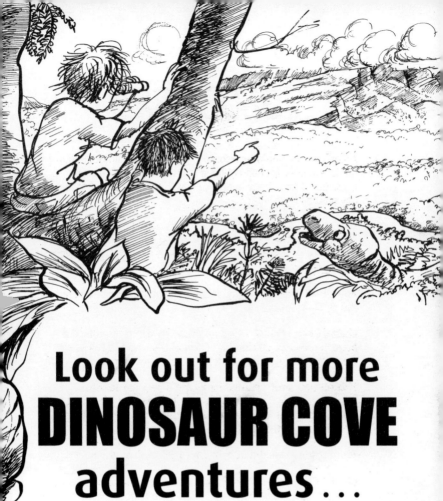

Look out for more
DINOSAUR COVE
adventures...

7 — DINOSAUR COVE — Rescuing the Plated Lizard — Rex Stone

8 — Rex Stone — DINOSAUR COVE — Swimming with the Sea Monster

9 — DINOSAUR COVE — Tracking the Gigantic Beast — Rex Stone

10 — Rex Stone — DINOSAUR COVE — Escape from the Fierce Predator

11 — Rex Stone — DINOSAUR COVE — Finding the Deceptive Dinosaur

12 — DINOSAUR COVE — Assault of the Friendly Fiends — Rex Stone

JURASSIC

Don't miss these fantastic double length Dinosaur Cove adventures

It's Christmas Eve in Dinosaur Cove and Jamie and Tom are off to their secret dino world. But the Jurassic jungle has disappeared and been replaced with snow! A new ice age world awaits them—blizzards, avalanches, a woolly mammoth in need of their help . . . and the boys' most amazing discovery **EVER!**

Jamie, Tom and Wanna are back in the Jurassic when disaster strikes! A pair of pterosaurs swoop down and grab Tom in their claws! How are Jamie and Wanna ever going to find him, especially now there's a pack of megalosaurs on the prowl? As Tom is carried away over the treetops, he wonders if he'll ever see his friends again . . .